THE DEVIL'S WALTZ

 This Large Print Book carries the Seal of Approval of N.A.V.H.

THE DEVIL'S WALTZ

ETHAN J. WOLFE

THORNDIKE PRESS
A part of Gale, a Cengage Company

Farmington Hills, Mich • San Francisco • New York • Waterville, Maine
Meriden, Conn • Mason, Ohio • Chicago

LIBRARY OF CONGRESS CIP DATA ON FILE.
CATALOGUING IN PUBLICATION FOR THIS BOOK
IS AVAILABLE FROM THE LIBRARY OF CONGRESS

ISBN-13: 978-1-4328-6133-9 (hardcover)

Published in 2019 by arrangement with Ethan J. Wolfe

Printed in the United States of America
1 2 3 4 5 6 7 23 22 21 20 19

For young authors who inspire me
and those who wear magic hats.

Chapter One

The train ride from Santa Fe to Yuma was close to unbearable. Fourteen hours of stifling heat from which even an open window didn't bring relief, never mind the stench of burning coal at every water stop along the way.

Scheduled for a ten a.m. arrival, the train was forty-five minutes late due to an unscheduled stop to grease wheels and pistons.

When US Marshal Dale Posey stepped off the train carrying his one satchel, the dry heat was like a slap in the face. May, and it had to be ninety degrees in the shade. He stood on the platform and looked at the town. About twelve hundred residents occupied the fairly large place, although the streets were close to deserted, and who could blame them in this heat.

Not far from town the Colorado River flowed, and was, about a thousand feet across at one point. A ferry boat took travelers across the river to California, panhandlers mostly, still seeking their elusive fortune in gold.

Dale set his satchel down for a moment to pull out his tobacco pouch and paper and roll a cigarette. He struck it with a match and inhaled with satisfaction. Sarah, his wife of eleven years, made him quit drinking the rye whiskey he enjoyed so much, but she couldn't make him quit the tobacco habit just yet.

Smoking, carrying the satchel, Dale stepped off the platform and walked the hundred yards or so to town.

Most of the shops, stores, and saloons were open for business, but few people were about. They were either all having an early lunch or avoiding the brutal heat. Dale bet on the heat.

He located the Yuma Hotel, a four-story structure with balconies on the front rooms. The lobby was spacious with several comfortable chairs, a long sofa with a table, and a small love seat. A few men sat reading newspapers and drinking coffee.

A clerk of about fifty with thinning brown hair stood behind the desk.

"Can I help you, sir?" he asked Dale.

"US Marshal Dale Posey," Dale said. "I wired to reserve a room."

"Oh yes, I have it right here," the clerk said. "I reserved room 403. It has a balcony facing Main Street."

"Can you have my bag brought up to the room and arrange for a bath for about an hour from now?" Dale said.

"Certainly, Marshal."

"Where is the sheriff's office?" Dale asked.

"Two streets to the left and one across."

"Back in an hour," Dale said.

He left the hotel, turned left, walked two blocks on the wood plank sidewalks, and crossed the street.

The sheriff's office was a stand-alone, red brick building with a heavy wood door and iron bars on the inside of a large plate-glass window.

Dale opened the door and stepped inside. Two men occupied the office, one seated at a desk, the other standing with a cup of coffee.

"I'm US Marshal Dale Posey," Dale said, looking at the man behind the desk. "Are you the sheriff?"

"I am going on eight years now. Name is Bill Riker. This is my deputy, James."

Dale looked at the deputy and noticed the resemblance.

"He your son?" Dale asked.

"He is and a good man," Riker said.

"Any more of that coffee you're drinking?" Dale asked.

James nodded and went to the woodstove.

"So what can I do for you, Marshal?" Riker asked.

"Have a good jail cell?"

"Best in the territory."

"Show me."

"May I ask your interest in my jail?" Riker asked.

Dale reached into the inside pocket of his jacket and produced a folded federal document and handed it to Riker.

"I'm extraditing a prisoner from Yuma and would like to pick him up this afternoon and have him spend the night in your jail so we can catch the ten o'clock train tomorrow morning," Dale said.

Riker scanned the paper, folded it, and gave it back to Dale.

"Jim," Riker said.

James handed Dale a tin mug of coffee and then opened a wood door that led to the two cells.

Dale followed him. The two cells were large enough to house four men each. Twin bunk beds, a sink, and toilet occupied each cell. Neither held a prisoner.

Dale and James returned to the office.

"Those will do just fine," Dale said.

"Yuma is a federal prison, and I ain't got much to do with it, but since I'll be holding one of their prisoners, I'd like to know who he is," Riker said.

"John Posey," Dale said.

Riker stared at Dale for a moment. "The one they call Jack, Lightning Jack?"

Dale nodded.

"He's also my kid brother," Dale said.

Dale shaved before immersing himself into a steaming hot tub of scented water. A Chinese woman the desk clerk called Mrs. Moy ran the hotel bathhouse. There were eight tubs, but Dale was the only one taking a bath at the time.

While he was soaping up, Mrs. Moy entered the bathhouse.

"You want haircut?" she asked in a thick accent.

"I could use one," Dale said. "When I get out."

"Best time when in water," Mrs. Moy said. "Hair wet."

Dale looked at her.

"I see many beans," Mrs. Moy said. "Thousands. Yours no different. Wash hair. I cut. Twenty-five cents extra."

"What the hell," Dale said.

■ ■ ■ ■

Freshly shaved, hair trimmed, Dale dug out a clean shirt from his satchel and pinned his badge to the left front pocket, then put it on. It was too damned hot for a jacket, so he wore just a vest.

As he stood before the mirror over the dresser, Dale strapped on his heavy gun belt. His sidearm of choice was a massive Smith & Wesson .44 revolver that weighed more than six pounds when loaded. The holster held eighteen bullets, which added even more weight to lug around on his waist.

Dale left the hotel and walked several blocks down a side street to a large livery stable. A burly blacksmith was hammering out shoes in front of a blistering fire. How the man stood the heat was a mystery.

"Stable manager around?" Dale asked the blacksmith.

"Office," the blacksmith said.

Dale turned and entered the stables where a small office was located on his right. A man was seated behind a desk, counting money.

"I need to rent a buggy for the day," Dale said.

"Where you headed?" the manager said.

He noticed the badge on Dale's shirt and added, "Marshal."

"The prison."

"Best take a team," the manager said. "In this heat a team lasts longer."

"Can you provide a fresh canteen?"

"Sure. For an extra dollar."

"I'm going to grab a quick lunch," Dale said. "Have the team ready when I get back."

"Eleven dollars in advance," the manager said. "You pay for what you break."

Yuma Prison came into view a quarter mile away. It was a huge structure, built to house five hundred prisoners at a time. Constructed of rock and cement with the heaviest iron bars available, it was conceived to be escape proof.

Even if you could escape, your choice was to flee to town and almost certain immediate capture, or flee into the desert and for certain die in that vast wilderness of scorched earth on foot.

As he neared the prison, guards on watchtowers observed him carefully. The front gates were open, and two armed guards stood watch on the outside.

Dale halted the team.

"US Marshal Dale Posey to see the warden," Dale said. He dug the folded letter of introduction for the warden and said, "Give this to the warden. I'll wait here."

Warden Fife was a short man in his late fifties. He met Dale in his office, which overlooked a courtyard where prisoners were cracking rocks with sledgehammers.

"May I offer you a cold drink, Marshal?" Fife asked when Dale was escorted into the office. "I'm partial to lemonade myself."

"That would be fine. Thank you."

"I must admit when I received the telegram from Washington, I was a bit taken aback," Fife said.

"Understandable," Dale said.

"Prisoner Posey is relations to you?" Fife said.

"My kid brother."

"I see. Where would you like to see him?"

"Someplace private."

"You'll need to check your firearm first."

The room was void of furniture. Fife said it was still under construction and would eventually be used as a dining hall for the guards.

When Dale entered the room, his brother, Jack Posey, was already inside and waiting.

His brother had always been taller than

him, taller than most, at six foot one inch in his bare feet, a good five inches taller than average for a man. Broad shouldered, heavily muscled, prison only seemed to add to his girth.

Shirtless, Posey was covered in sweat and grime and he looked at Dale.

"Prison seems to agree with you, Jack," Dale said. "You look fine. Why's your hair so short?"

Posey's sandy-colored hair was worn close to the scalp.

"Head lice," Posey said. "They like long hair and beards."

Dale walked close to his brother and had to look up to see him eye-to-eye.

"Been pounding rock, by the look of your hands," Dale said.

"Eight hours a day, six days a week," Posey said.

Dale nodded. Then he punched Posey on the jaw as hard as he could.

Posey's knees buckled, but he didn't go down.

"Stupid son of a bitch," Dale said and punched his brother again, and again his brother stayed on his feet.

Posey waited for his head to clear and looked at Dale.

"Did you get that out of your system?"

15

Posey asked.

Dale shook the pain out of his right hand. "Got any possessions or money?"

"A clean work shirt and pants and seventeen dollars," Posey said.

"Go back to your cell and get your shirt. You're coming with me," Dale said.

"Where?" Posey asked.

"Wherever I say," Dale said.

CHAPTER TWO

His arms and legs shackled, Posey was dumped onto the back of the buggy by two guards.

"Obliged," Dale said to them.

"Is this necessary?" Posey asked.

"You shut your mouth and keep it shut until I tell you to open it," Dale said.

Posey grinned at the guards as Dale yanked the reins and the buggy lurched forward.

When they rode into Yuma late in the day, the streets were full of citizens. Most stopped whatever they were doing to watch the wagon with Dale driving and the filthy prisoner in back roll into town.

Dale stopped the wagon in front of the hotel.

As Dale stepped down, Sheriff Riker and James crossed the street and approached the buggy.

"Good Lord," Riker said.

"As soon as I get him cleaned up, he's yours for the night, Sheriff," Dale said.

"Even upwind I can smell him," Riker said.

"I'd like to borrow your deputy for a bit," Dale said.

Posey sat in a tub of hot, soapy water as Mrs. Moy shaved his face.

"Wash hair good," she said. "Very dirty."

Posey grinned as he looked at James, who stood in the corner, watching.

"I don't suppose a man could get a shot of something to drink around here?" he asked.

"I can't abide giving a prisoner liquor," James said.

"Hold still," Mrs. Moy said. "Cut face."

Posey waited until she had scraped the last bit of soap off his face and then he dunked under the water to rinse off. When he came back up, Dale was there and said, "Is he clean?"

"Clean enough," she said.

"Good," Dale said and tossed his brother a wrapped package. "Get dressed."

Dressed in new trail clothing that consisted of black shirt and pants, new boots and hat,

Posey walked across the street in shackles to the jail.

Dale and James escorted him.

Once Posey was safely in a cell, Dale removed the shackles.

"James, can you ask the restaurant across the street to bring two steaks with all the trimmings and a pot of coffee to the jail?" Dale said.

"Hey, and some apple pie," Posey said. "I haven't had apple pie in three years."

Dale nodded to James.

James left the back room.

"So what's this all about, Dale?" Posey asked.

Dale rolled a cigarette as he looked at Posey.

"Can you fix one for me?" Posey asked.

Dale gave him the cigarette and rolled a second. He lit both off one wood match.

"That's good," Posey said.

"Virginia tobacco," Dale said.

"So why am I here, big brother?" Posey asked.

"You owe me twenty-three dollars for the clothing," Dale said.

Posey sat on a bed. "You going to charge me for the steak, too?"

"That comes under the feed and care of a

prisoner," Dale said. "I'll be back when the steaks arrive."

Dale had Fife open the door so a table with two chairs could be brought into the cell. Two oil lanterns provided enough light to read by as well as eat.

"Last time I had a steak was the last time I had a drink of rye whiskey," Posey said.

James came into the cell.

"Want me to stand guard?" James asked.

"Why?" Dale said. "Do you think my brother is going to steal my baked potato?"

"Okay, then," James said. "I'll be in the office if you need me."

The brothers sliced into their steaks and began to eat.

"You have eight more years left on your sentence," Dale said. "Eight more years of back-breaking hard labor. You'll be. What? Forty-four years old by the time you see daylight."

Posey ate a hunk of steak and washed it down with a sip of coffee.

"I heard they killed old Jesse James a few months back," he said. "I never did like old Jesse. Now his brother Frank, now there was a thinking man."

"Are you listening to me, Jack?" Dale asked.

"Killed William Bonney, locked up John Hardin, and I hear Holliday is off somewhere dying of consumption."

"Dammit, Jack, listen to me," Dale said.

Posey cut and ate another piece of steak. "I'm listening."

"I have a document here signed by the governor of Arizona Territory and the President himself," Dale said. "To grant you a full pardon."

Posey stared at his brother for a moment. "Full pardon?"

"Expunging you of all and any crimes of your past," Dale said.

"And what do I have to do to earn such high regard from the governor of Arizona Territory and President?"

"Help me find and capture Tom Spooner," Dale said.

Posey looked at Dale without expression. Then his lips curled into a smile and he cracked up laughing.

"You're crazy," Posey said.

"The day of the outlaw is coming to an end, Jack," Dale said. "They have telephones and electric lights in New York. Electrified trains that run underground. Indoor toilets even. The west needs to be settled, and dangerous men like Spooner put away."

"This ain't New York, and you're not good

enough to take Tom Spooner," Posey said.

"But you are," Dale said. "And you're going to help me or rot in Yuma another eight years. The choice is yours, Jack."

"Jesus, Dale," Posey said. "Tom Spooner."

"I know how you feel, Jack. I liked old Tom myself that time I met him, and I know you rode a lot of miles together, but he's not fit to ride free anymore," Dale said. "Now make your choice. If I leave here without your signature, the deal is off the table and I'll see you in another eight years."

"It won't be easy smoking old Tom out," Posey said. "And if we do find him, he won't go quietly."

"The warrant says dead or alive," Dale said.

Posey sighed.

"I said, make your choice," Dale said.

"Total pardon?" Posey said.

"The minute we reach Santa Fe."

"Why Santa Fe?"

"I'm federal, but I'm assigned to New Mexico Territory," Dale said. "That will be our starting point once I send the signed document to Washington. Once I send it off, my authority covers all United States and territories."

"I think I read about that in the newspapers."

"So what's it going to be, Jack?"

"Eight years is a long time," Posey said.

"It is that," Dale said.

"What about the farm?" Posey asked.

"It's still there. Hasn't been worked since 'sixty-five, but the land is good," Dale said. "I pay the taxes on it every year."

"Well, I'm glad you didn't sell it," Posey said.

"Yes or no, Jack. The offer is good until midnight tonight, like the paper says."

Posey sighed. "Got a pen and ink?" he said.

CHAPTER THREE

Dale left Posey the pouch of tobacco, papers and matches, and coffee pot and cup, but the deputy removed the oil lanterns before locking the cell.

Light filtered in through the barred window from the nearly full moon and the lit lanterns in the hallway leading to the office.

Posey rolled a cigarette and sipped coffee from the tin cup as he stretched out on a lower bunk.

He felt his mind start to wander and he let the thoughts flow at will.

His parents, John and Mary Kate Posey, migrated from Ireland to America in eighteen forty, the first of the Posey family to leave the homeland. They arrived by boat in New York City with the clothes on their back and their life savings of one thousand dollars.

The Irish relocation organization helped them find a small farm in southern Missouri near the Arkansas border. Three hundred acres of good farmland. With little left of their savings after purchasing the property, John and Mary Kate went to work building a new life.

In eighteen forty-two, they brought in their first crop along with the hogs John raised on the side.

That was the year Dale was born.

By eighteen forty-eight, the year John, Jr., entered the world, the Posey farm was prosperous and growing and had done so without the need for slaves like in the neighboring states of Arkansas and Tennessee.

Dale was highly book smart and was sent to the agricultural college in Vermont to study the latest developments in farming. That was in eighteen sixty, when Dale was just eighteen years old.

Less than a year later, the War Between the States broke out.

In early 'sixty-three, when Dale was but twenty-one years old, he was commissioned a First Lieutenant in the 1st Cavalry Regiment. He first saw action in the Battle of Big Bethel. In July, Dale's unit fought at Gettysburg and helped stop the charge of General Pickett.

Soon after Gettysburg, Posey left home to

join the fight. Although he wasn't yet sixteen, he was nearly six feet tall and had the girth of a man. He had little trouble lying about his age and enlisted into the Union Army in Illinois. Taught by his father, young Posey was an expert marksman and was sent to a special unit assigned to guard General Sherman.

While serving in the special unit, Posey met a young soldier from central Missouri named Tom Spooner. A few years older than Posey, Spooner had an easy way about him and a winning smile that set you at ease. But when the fighting started, Spooner was as deadly as any man anywhere.

In November of 'sixty-four, along with sixty thousand Union soldiers, Posey and Spooner followed General Sherman as he marched to the sea.

Complete destruction of everything in their path.

Sherman said his goal was to break the back of the south, and that is exactly what they did, burning and destroying farms, entire towns, the city of Atlanta, and every Confederate soldier encountered along the way.

When the devastation was complete, Posey and Spooner continued to serve with Sherman until Lee's surrender in April of 'sixty-five.

Not even a week after the surrender, Lincoln was assassinated.

In June of 'sixty-five, Posey and Spooner, both sergeants upon discharge, rode horses provided by the cavalry west and home to Missouri.

Dale, now a major, stayed in the army to help the south with reconstruction.

In early August, when they reached the Missouri line, Posey and Spooner decided to ride to Posey's farm first and then travel north to Spooner's.

What they didn't know was that, while they were away, a civil war in Missouri broke out between those who wanted to stay loyal to the Union and those opposed. Raiders loyal to the south from Arkansas came across the border and murdered and destroyed hundreds of farms and their occupants.

Posey and Spooner found the Posey farmhouse burned to the ground as well as the barn and corral. Posey's parents were buried in a field behind where the house once stood. They rode to town and spoke with the law, an old, useless sheriff. He told them it was Rebel raiders who did it in late 'sixty-four, riding across the border at night. He wouldn't know who to arrest for the crimes or he surely would have.

They rode north a hundred miles to the Spooner farm and found the same: a house burned to the ground, his entire family butchered, including Spooner's eleven-year-old baby sister.

They rode to Springfield to see the federal law, but got the same story about raiders and there was nothing they could do about it without knowing who the men responsible were.

Posey set out to find his brother, Dale. He heard he was in Georgia with the reconstruction of the South project. Having nowhere to go at that time, Spooner went with him, and they arrived in Atlanta in late September.

They found Dale camped outside of Atlanta with the regiment assigned to oversee the reconstruction of the city.

Carpetbaggers were everywhere, promising forty acres and a mule to freed slaves who didn't know how to read, much less farm using modern-day methods.

Posey was shocked to learn that Dale knew what happened back home in 'sixty-four, having been notified by mail from surviving neighbors. The army wasn't about to release men, much less an officer, to return home to see to family matters, so

Dale saw no reason to inform his brother.

"It would only lead you to worry and get yourself killed in combat, or worse, make a deserter out of you," Dale had said. "I figured you'd find out soon enough when you got home."

"I don't know about you, Jack," Spooner said later on. "But I know what I'm going to do."

Not yet nineteen, a veteran of the war, and a decorated sergeant under General Sherman, Posey found himself riding with a group of men put together by Spooner. Each man, a Missouri volunteer who fought for the Union, had come home to similar circumstances.

Revenge was Spooner's objective.

It became theirs.

Since there was no one man or group to take their revenge upon, they targeted the southern railroads, stagecoaches, and banks, robbing any and all. They never crossed into the northern line and rarely had to use violence.

At first.

By 'sixty-eight, the group had amassed a tidy sum of money and valuables and was now wanted by not only the law, but the army as well.

Men like Custer and Bat Masterson were

on their trail.

Then came the bounty hunters. Hard men, most of them ex-soldiers on both sides, left without a profession other than killing for cash reward.

In late 'sixty-nine, after the group had successfully robbed three southern banks, several stagecoaches, and one train, they were forced into hiding by a large band of bounty hunters.

Spooner suggested they ride south into Florida and hide out in the panhandle. Pensacola proved to be a right nice place. No one knew them and Posey, Spooner, and the boys spent many pleasant afternoons lounging at the beach and swimming in the warm oceanfront.

It was late spring when the band of bounty hunters caught up with them. The group had rented a small cabin outside of town and the bounty hunters struck at dawn.

A bloody battle ensued between Posey, Spooner, and their four men, and the dozen bounty hunters that attacked.

The bounty hunters figured they would have an easy time of it, but Posey posted two lookouts on the roof and they were prepared.

Much blood was spilled.

By noon, just Spooner and Posey were

alive inside the cabin, and seven bounty hunters lay dead.

Posey offered the bounty hunters a truce, but they refused. The bounty money was too good to walk away from.

While Spooner provided cover with a Henry rifle, Posey went out a back window and climbed up to the roof with a .50 caliber Sharps rifle, the weapon he carried in the army.

With the Sharps, Posey killed the remaining five bounty hunters, two of them when running away.

Posey and Spooner had no choice but to take what supplies they could carry and leave the dead men where they lay.

Posey wanted to go south to Miami.

Spooner felt going south would leave them with no escape route if more bounty hunters got on their trail.

They rode north into Georgia, avoiding towns, cities, and farms. They grew out their hair and beards to disguise their faces. Near Albany, Georgia, they found a general store by the Chattahoochee River and loaded up on supplies. They rode a ferry across the river and continued riding west into Alabama.

There was little love of Yankees in Alabama, and they were able to hide out for close to a year in relative comfort. They moved around a lot, often switching between the northern part of the state and the southern tip.

Money wasn't a problem. They had stolen a fortune and lived like common folk.

Then, in late 'seventy-one, Spooner got the itch. He wanted to go back to work robbing the south for what they did to his family.

Posey told him things had changed in six years. The south had been rebuilt with northern money. There was no one left to enact their revenge upon, if there ever had been.

Posey secretly believed Spooner just wanted to rob and steal for the sake of doing it, but he wasn't about to leave his partner and friend to go it alone.

The Southern Pacific Railroad was too big and powerful for the two of them to take on, and recruiting new men sympathetic to their cause was nearly impossible anymore. They went small, holding up stagecoaches and ferryboats and the occasional bank if it was small enough.

By early 'seventy-two, they were on the run again when the Overland and other stage lines offered rewards for their capture.

They fled west to southern Oklahoma and

hid in the mountains of the Indian Territory. There they met Big Nose Kate, a notorious prostitute who years later became famous when she took up with Doc Holliday. They liked Kate, and she took them in for a while as they regrouped.

Then, in late 'seventy-two, Posey read several stories in the *Arkansas Ledger Newspaper* that changed his course. The first story concerned his brother, Dale. After four years as a US deputy marshal in Missouri, he was appointed to the rank of US marshal in New Mexico Territory.

Posey had no idea his older brother was the law, never mind now a full US marshal. He had assumed incorrectly that Dale had returned to the farm.

The other story concerned the Pinkerton detectives. The firm of experienced lawmen and trackers had been hired by various stagecoach lines, railroad lines, and even some banks to track down and bring in as many outlaws as possible.

Posey suggested it was time to leave Oklahoma and ride north, possibly to Montana or the Dakotas where they weren't known, and start living as honest men.

Spooner wasn't having any of that. He wanted to stay with Big Nose Kate until things quieted down, although he bore no ill will toward Posey for his decision. Posey stayed on one more winter before his decision came to a head.

In spring of 'seventy-four, when the mountain snow melted and the days grew warm, Spooner and Posey parted ways.

Posey rode west and north into Kansas, where he took work on several cattle drives for various ranches herding beef.

Come winter, he'd ride down to Texas and wait out the cold weather near the Gulf or in Austin. He rode to the farm in Missouri and was shocked to see it deserted.

Time seemed to slip away, especially when working cattle drives or the occasional fence-mending assignment. Two winters he spent in a linemen's shack in Colorado, a bleak and lonely job.

In the summer of 'seventy-nine, his crimes finally caught up with him.

Years earlier, when Posey and Spooner were hiding in Alabama, Posey saw the most unique handgun he'd ever come across. A striking black Colt Peacemaker with black ivory grips. Carved into the ivory was the image of a hooded cobra snake about to strike.

The weapon was custom-made for a rich rancher who'd died before he could pick it up. Posey purchased the gun for the very stiff price of one hundred and twenty-five dollars.

When he was working horses for the Big Whiskey Ranch in Arizona Territory, six Pinkerton detectives rode in and surrounded Posey as he was gathering strays. A local ranch foreman recognized Posey's unique Peacemaker from a stagecoach he had been on when it was robbed and sent a wire to the detective agency. He later collected the five-thousand-dollar reward, but six months later was shot in the back and killed.

Dale attended Posey's trial held in the capital city of Phoenix.

That was the first time Posey had seen his brother in more than a decade, and he didn't see him again until yesterday.

It was nine years since Posey parted ways with Spooner. Every now and then, he would catch a snippet of news about Spooner when working a drive somewhere. The latest bank he robbed or stagecoach he held up with his new band of men. On several occasions, Spooner killed members of a posse in pursuit.

Killing lawmen was a sure way to a hanging.

Posey rolled and smoked another cigarette as he thought.

Smoking old Tom out was going to be a daunting task. He was as skilled as any man with a gun or at tracking, was totally fearless, and, most of all, and what Dale didn't realize, was that Tom Spooner was completely insane.

Posey could see the madness slowly come on and take over Spooner's mind piece by piece. Little things at first, like planning more dangerous jobs than were necessary so his men would be in more danger than need be.

After a while, Posey realized what Spooner was actually looking for was a reason to kill.

A man who looks for reasons to kill when none existed is just plumb crazy.

And the odds of taking Spooner alive were less than zero.

CHAPTER FOUR

Sheriff Riker woke Posey at seven in the morning with a cup of coffee and a basin of water for him to wash up in.

Around seven thirty, Riker and his deputy, James, returned with a table and two chairs and brought them into the cell. A few minutes later, Dale and a full breakfast prepared by the hotel arrived.

"Eat hardy, Jack," Dale said. "We got a long train ahead of us this morning."

Fried eggs, bacon and potatoes, toast, juice, and coffee with some kind of pastry Posey had never seen before but tasted delicious.

Dale called it a Danish.

"Train leaves at ten," Dale said. "We'll be in Santa Fe around midnight."

"I gave this some serious consideration last night," Posey said as he sopped up the runny part of an egg with toast. "Old Tom won't go easy. You're going to have to kill

37

him. He won't go alive, for sure."

"Maybe with you along you could talk some sense into him," Dale said.

"Remember that story Ma used to tell us as kids about the mouse that fell into the bucket of cream?" Posey said.

Dale shook his head. "I don't recall."

"This little mouse smells the fresh cream and climbs into the bucket," Posey said. "Once he's inside he realizes he's going to drown. He's left with two choices. Accept his fate and drown or fight like hell to survive. So the little mouse fights like hell to live. He fought and fought and fought so hard he churned the cream into butter and then climbed out of the bucket alive and well. That's Tom Spooner."

"Maybe so, but we won't be going after him with a bucket of cream," Dale said. "Finish your breakfast. We have a train to catch."

Dale and Posey stood on the platform at nine forty-five and waited for the ten o'clock train to arrive.

A dozen or more passengers waiting for the train stared at the shackles around Posey's legs and wrists.

"Is this necessary?" Posey asked as he shook his wrists and the shackles clanked.

"It is until we reach Santa Fe and the pardon takes effect," Dale said.

"Well, roll me a cigarette then," Posey said.

Dale rolled two, lit them both with a wood match, and gave one to Posey.

"Thank you kindly, brother," Posey said.

Dale looked at his pocket watch. "Damn train better be on time."

"Is that Pa's old watch?" Posey asked.

"It is," Dale said. "Came all the way from Ireland with him. He gave it to me when I went into the army."

"I remember every night after supper he would wind that watch and set it open-faced on the mantle above the fireplace," Posey said.

"I remember," Dale said.

Looking down the tracks, Posey spotted the arriving train.

"What did you finish up with when you got out?" Posey asked.

"Lieutenant Colonel," Dale said.

"That made it easy to get appointed marshal, huh?"

"Nothing easy about being a marshal," Dale said.

"Pay is good?"

"Jack, be quiet. The train is almost here."

After a while, the constant rocking motion

of the train lulled Posey to sleep in his window seat.

Dale made provisions so that it was just the two of them in the first car for the other passengers' safety. The slowing of the train woke Posey, and he opened his eyes when the train stopped.

"Water stop," Dale said.

"Where are we?"

"About a hundred miles east of Yuma."

Dale had a Bible on his lap. It was well-worn and tattered.

"Is that Ma's Bible?" Posey asked.

"It is."

"She read to us from it every night," Posey said.

"I remember," Dale said. "She gave it to me before I left for the army. She said to carry it into battle and it would protect me."

"And did it?"

"I'm still here."

"Matthew, chapter seven, do unto others as they would do unto you," Posey said. "Only do it first and don't miss. That's Tom Spooner."

"A two-bit outlaw, thief, and murderer, that's Tom Spooner, Jack," Dale said.

"I'm no better," Posey said.

"Maybe not," Dale said. "We'll see. In the meantime, be quiet."

Posey looked out the window as the train started to roll forward.

Once the train was at full speed, the door to the car opened and a porter entered.

"The dining car opens at one if you and your . . . if you would like to have lunch," the porter said.

"I would, but could you arrange to have it brought here?" Dale said.

"For two?" the porter asked.

"Yes," Dale said.

Posey grinned at the porter. "Maybe something a bit more high-spirited than coffee to drink," he said.

"No spirits served until after four," the porter said.

"Coffee will be fine," Dale said.

Posey opened his eyes and looked out the window at the darkness and said, "Where are we now?"

"Maybe an hour from Santa Fe," Dale said. "I swear, Jack, you sleep more than any man I've ever seen."

"Nothing else to do," Posey said. "Roll me a smoke, would you."

"I'm going for some coffee first," Dale said. "Be right back."

Posey watched the darkness outside his window while Dale was gone and thought if it was anybody but his brother, he'd be long gone by now. But he gave Dale his word, and he'd be hard-pressed to break it.

Dale returned with two cups of coffee. He set them on the floor and rolled two cigarettes, then gave cup and cigarette to Posey.

"Two hundred and fifty dollars plus expenses," Dale said.

Posey looked at his brother.

"That's what a US marshal makes every month," Dale said.

"It ain't enough," Posey said.

"We're coming into the station soon," Dale said. "Finish your coffee."

Walking off the train, Posey stretched his back as best he could with the heavy shackles still binding his legs and wrists.

It was after midnight, and they were the only two exiting the train.

Two US deputy marshals waited with shotguns on the platform.

"Take these damn things off me, Dale," Posey said.

"Sure," Dale said. "As soon as you're safely locked in a cell for the night."

"You said in Santa Fe . . ." Posey said.

"As soon as I send the papers in the morning," Dale said. "In the meantime, breakfast is served at seven thirty sharp."

"Son of a bitch," Posey said.

Grinning, Dale said, "Go easy on him, boys. He's a big, dumb, son of a bitch, but he's the only brother I got."

The marshal's office was large enough to accommodate three desks, one for Dale and one for each of his two deputies. The jail cells, three in all, could hold as many as six men per cell.

Posey found himself alone in the first cell.

As one deputy stood by with a shotgun, the other deputy removed the shackles.

" 'Cause a you, I gotta sleep in the office tonight instead a next to my nice, warm wife," the shotgun-toting deputy said.

"Try breaking rocks at Yuma, you big dandy," Posey said.

"If you weren't Dale's brother, I'd pound you to sand," the deputy said.

At least six inches taller than the deputy, Posey grinned and said, "Make sure you wake me at seven." Then he sat on a cot and added, "Shorty."

CHAPTER FIVE

A deputy woke Posey exactly at seven o'clock.

"Got a mug of coffee and fresh water for washing," the deputy said.

Once the basin and coffee were inside the cell, Posey stuck his head, hair and all, into the fresh, cold water. The deputy handed him a small towel when Posey emerged from the basin.

He wiped his face clean, ran his fingers through his close-cropped hair, and then took the mug of coffee.

"You're free to come out and wait in the office with us," the deputy said. "The marshal should be here any minute."

"Thank you kindly," Posey said.

He followed the deputy to the office where the other deputy sat behind a desk.

"Mind if I sit?" Posey said and sat on the corner of Dale's desk.

"I don't understand none of this and,

44

personally, I think the marshal is crazy letting you loose like this," the seated deputy said.

Posey rolled a cigarette and said, "Have you had any luck catching Tom Spooner?"

"You know we ain't," the standing deputy said.

"Got a match?" Posey asked.

The standing deputy dug a wood match out of a shirt pocket and handed it to Posey.

"Thanks," Posey said, then struck the match against the desk and lit the cigarette.

"So you think you can catch Tom Spooner?" the seated deputy said.

"My brother does," Posey said. "That's what matters."

"I'd like to get you alone in that cell back there, we'll see . . ." the standing deputy said.

The door opened and Dale walked in with a wrapped package under his arm.

"We'll see what?" Dale asked.

"Nothing," the standing deputy said.

Dale tossed the package to Posey. "Clean shirt. Put it on."

"Two clean shirts in three days," Posey said. "This keeps up and I'll be a dandy soon . . . like your deputies."

■ ■ ■ ■

A buggy waited in front of the office and Posey remarked, "Is my big brother going soft that he rides around in a buggy?"

"Belongs to my wife, Sarah," Dale said. "We been married going on eleven years now."

"You didn't mention her before," Posey said.

"I'm mentioning her now," Dale said. "We're going to my home, and I expect you to act accordingly. Sarah is the preacher over at the church, and she doesn't take kindly to cussing and liquor."

"You married a preacher lady," Posey said. "Jesus, Dale."

"Met right after the war during the reconstruction," Dale said. "I knew right off she was for me, but she took some convincing."

As Dale drove the buggy along Main Street, they passed under a long banner hung between two buildings on opposite sides of the street. The banner read *See Dan Brouthers and the Buffalo Bisons play John Morrill and the Boston Beaneaters. Today. Admission twenty-five cents.*

"What's that about?" Posey asked.

"Remember the game the soldiers would

46

play to pass the time?" Dale said. "The game with the stick and ball. They called it baseball."

"I remember," Posey said. "I played it a few times myself."

"They play it for money now. There'll be a game today in the field north of town."

"Play for money?" Posey said. "Who would pay to see that?"

Dale turned the buggy onto Oak Street and continued until they reached the last house. It was a large home with yellow shutters and gray trim, a fenced-in garden out front, and a swing set on the porch.

"This is my house," Dale said.

Posey and Dale stepped down from the buggy and walked to the porch. The door opened and Sarah Posey stepped out to meet them. She wore a simple white dress with a high collar and had her golden hair worn up in a bun, but Posey thought her a striking-looking woman.

"Sarah, this is my brother, Jack," Dale said.

Sarah smiled at Posey. "Welcome," she said.

"Where are the . . . ?" Dale said.

"Right here," Sarah said, and their two children stepped out from behind her.

"My daughter is Erin," Dale said. "She's eight."

She was cute as a button with sandy-colored hair and a tiny, upturned nose.

"Erin, this is your Uncle Jack," Dale said.

"Hello, sir," Erin said.

"Erin was our ma's name," Posey said.

"I know that, sir," Erin said.

"The boy is John, and he's all of nine," Dale said.

"John, is it?" Posey said and looked at Dale.

He was a scrawny boy but showed promise.

"My father told me you were with General Sherman during the war," John said.

"Right true," Posey said.

"For goodness' sake, everybody, come in to breakfast," Sarah said.

After breakfast, Dale and Posey took coffee on the porch, where they both rolled cigarettes.

Sarah came out with the pot to refill their cups.

"I wish you'd quit that habit, Dale," Sarah said. "And it's doing you no good either, Jack."

"Yes, ma'am," Posey said. "That was a right elegant breakfast, and your blessing was beautifully said."

"You haven't heard anything yet, Jack," Dale said.

"As soon as you're done with your coffee, hitch the second buggy," Sarah said.

"Yes, ma'am," Dale said.

As soon as Sarah was inside the house, Posey said, "Are we going somewhere?"

"Church," Dale said. "Today is Sunday."

The church was the last structure on Main Street at the very edge of town. Santa Fe had a large population of six thousand, and Posey swore every last one of them was in church that Sunday morning.

Posey wasn't sure if that was because Santa Fe was full of sinners who needed the word of God, or because that word of God was being delivered by a strikingly beautiful woman all fired up and red in the cheeks.

Posey suspected the latter.

After the hour-long sermon, Sarah and Dale stood on the top steps and greeted the faithful as they flocked out of the church.

Posey waited by the buggy.

When the last of the faithful had left the church, Dale came down to the buggy.

"Sarah and the kids are going home," Dale said. "You come with me to the office."

■ ■ ■ ■

Using a key, Dale unlocked the gun safe against the wall in his office.

"What's your fancy?" he asked.

Posey inspected the long guns.

"The Winchester 75 with the adjustable sights," Posey said. "And that Sharps will do nicely."

"Can you still hit anything?" Dale asked.

Posey looked at Dale and Dale said, "Well, it's been two years since you shot anything."

"The warden at Yuma likes fresh meat," Posey said. "With a team of guards, I used to hunt for him once or twice a week. They let me use an old Springfield rifle, and I could still take the eye out of a rabbit mid-hop. I'd be allowed one bullet at a time and I never missed. What can I have for a short gun?"

Dale went to his desk and opened the wide bottom drawer. He removed a black gun belt wrapped around the holster and tossed it to Posey.

"By God, that's my Colt," Posey said.

"I saved it from your trial," Dale said. "Cleaned and oiled just last week."

Posey pulled the Colt from the holster and held the black handgun in his right hand. It was like shaking hands with an old, trusted friend.

"Okay, let's go," Dale said.

"Where?"

"I like to select my tools carefully for each job," Dale said.

A few blocks from the office, down Elm Street at the very end of the block, stood a private livery stable and corral. A sign on the stable read, *US Marshal's Service Use Only.*

An old man in his sixties greeted them at the corral.

"Howdy, Marshal," the old man said.

"Jack, this here is Pete Thompson," Dale said. "Pete served as Grant's personal horse groomer during the war. If he doesn't know it about a horse, it's because there's nothing left to know. Pete, my brother, Jack Posey."

Pete gave Posey a once-over. "You got the look of a Sherman man to me," he said.

"Rode with the general two years," Posey said.

"We need two horses for a long and hard ride," Dale said.

"Them there in the corral are all first-rate, but I got two inside I been working on since they got here a few months ago," Pete said.

Dale and Posey followed Pete inside the

livery where two massive black horses stood side-by-side in a stall.

"They're fifteen hand and strong as oxes," Pete said. "Brothers from different mothers, but they dad is pure."

"Saddle them," Dale said. "Best saddles and bags we got. We'll take them out for a little ride."

The horses had little trouble adjusting to Dale and Posey, and they rode ten miles south of town without either horse breaking a sweat.

They rode to the Santa Fe River, which had been dammed in 'eighty-one to provide water to two reservoirs for the town's use. They followed the riverbed for several more miles and dismounted near some trees.

While the horses grazed on grass, Dale and Posey sat in the shade of a tall tree.

Each man rolled a cigarette and lit them off wood matches.

"You got the chance for a new start, Jack. A new life," Dale said. "I'm not saying you should go back to the farm, but at least you can make something of yourself while you're still young. Maybe find a good woman like Sarah and settle down."

"Settle down to what?" Posey asked.

"Just settle down," Dale said. "I know you

did most of what you did out of some sort of justice for the war, but it's long in the past, and you must have realized it was fruitless or you wouldn't have parted ways with Tom."

Posey watched the horses graze for a bit.

"I would like to see the farm one more time though," he said.

"After this trip, you're free to do as you please," Dale said.

"If Tom don't kill the both of us," Posey said.

Dale grinned and said, "Let's go back. We still have some work to do."

Seated at his desk with his two deputies and Posey standing, Dale opened a large map.

"Is that coffee hot?" Dale asked a deputy.

"Just made," the deputy said.

"Pour us all a cup and then come in close," Dale said.

The deputy filled four mugs and passed them around.

"I marked in red pencil where Tom Spooner has struck in the last six months," Dale said.

Posey looked at the map.

"Jesus, Dale, that's near thirty robberies," Posey said.

"Thirty-three to be exact," Dale said.

53

"He's held up everything from the stage-coach taking passengers to Denver to catch the train, to banks, a mining payroll, and even a train out of Wyoming where he and his men rode as passengers."

"Where's the last jobs he's pulled?" Posey asked.

"A little bank in Grayson in southern Utah," Dale said.

"Utah?" Posey said. "It appears Tom's days of robbing to punish the south are over."

"Been over for a long time now, Jack," Dale said.

"How many men he ride with?"

"Some say as many as fifteen."

"Is he killing?"

"Everywhere he goes."

Posey studied the map closely. "How far apart are the jobs pulled?"

"Seems like every two weeks or so," Dale said.

"Are you figuring we should start in Grayson?" Posey asked.

"Unless I get reports he struck in the last few days, Grayson is as good a place as any to start," Dale said.

Posey took a sip of coffee. "Okay," he said.

After a quiet dinner, Dale and Posey took

coffee to the porch and sat in the cool of the evening.

They rolled and smoked cigarettes.

"We'll catch the train north to Alamosa and then west to the Utah line and ride the rest of the way," Dale said.

"We'll need supplies," Posey said.

"Whatever we need we'll get in Alamosa."

Holding a mug of coffee, Sarah came out to the porch and took the chair next to Dale.

"I packed a bedroll for each of you," she said. "An extra shirt and socks, needle and thread and a pint of whiskey for emergency use."

Sarah paused and looked at Dale.

"And I do mean emergency use," she said.

"Of course," Dale said.

"That means you, too," Sarah said to Posey.

"Wouldn't dream of touching the stuff unless I was snake bit," Posey said.

Sarah nodded. "Well, all right then," she said. "Dale, you don't stay up too late."

"Be in shortly," Dale said.

After Sarah went inside, Posey said, "You know why Tom hits every two weeks?"

"I thought on it, but no, I don't," Dale admitted.

"He's got a centralized hiding place that's a two-week ride in any direction," Posey

55

said. "It's how we did it in the old days. Plan the job around the escape route and hide out."

"Makes sense."

"Do you know I read in a newspaper in Yuma Prison that they got houses in New York and Boston with the bathtubs right inside this little room?" Posey said.

"I do. What's that got to do with anything?"

"Nothing," Posey said. "I just want to live long enough to see one of them."

Chapter Six

In the morning, Dale brought freshly laundered clothes to the guestroom where Posey slept.

"These are my old trail clothes and hat," Posey said.

"I saved them after your trial," Dale said. "Hurry up and get dressed. Breakfast is waiting."

Erin and John watched as their father and uncle strapped on their guns. They had watched their father put on his holster hundreds of times as he readied for work. It just seemed natural, like he was putting on his vest or hat.

But the way their uncle put on his holster was different. He did it with such ease that the holster and gun became like a part of him. Once the holster was on, he adjusted it slightly and then gently lifted the gun up a bit as if testing the action of the holster.

Even though they were just kids, Erin and John realized that something was different about their uncle.

He looked at them and grinned.

Then they realized what it was that was different.

Their uncle was a very dangerous man.

Sarah came out on the porch.

"I'm taking the buggy to give your father and uncle a ride to the livery," she said. "The dishes best be clean when I return."

"Yes, Ma," Erin said.

"John?" Sarah said.

"Yes, Ma," John said.

"Well, both you men, let's go," Sarah said. "The livery isn't coming to us."

Sarah stood beside the buggy and waited for Dale and Posey to bring their horses out of the livery.

Old Pete was at the corral, chewing tobacco and spitting up a storm.

"Look like we might finally get some rain," he said with tobacco juice dribbling down his chin.

"Shut up, you old fool," Sarah said. "And I best see you at next Sunday service and without a mouthful of tobacco juice."

"Yes, ma'am," Pete said.

Posey led his horse out first and stood

beside the corral so Dale could lead his horse past him to the buggy.

Posey watched silently while his brother and Sarah said a few words, then kissed and hugged.

Dale mounted then, but Sarah surprised Posey by walking to him.

"You make sure nothing happens to him," she said.

"I will," Posey said.

"Dale is a good man," Sarah said. "His children need him. I need him. You make sure or don't come back."

"Yes, ma'am," Posey said as he mounted up.

Sarah returned to the buggy and watched as Dale and Posey rode off to catch the train to Grayson.

After six hours on the train, Posey and Dale stretched out their backs on the Alamosa platform before getting the horses from the boxcar.

"Let's check in with the sheriff and grab a hot lunch," Dale said. "It may be our last for a while."

Alamosa was established just a few years earlier as a railway center for train repairs. It had a population of around eight hundred citizens, of which all but around fifty worked for the railroad.

The law was a member of the railroad police and had an office in the center of town.

"I'm US Marshal Dale Posey," Dale said when he entered the office.

"Ed Davis, Chief of Railroad Police for Alamosa. My deputies are out with a repair crew."

"I'm after Tom Spooner and his bunch," Dale said. "Me and my man outside there with the horses."

"Just the two of you after that bunch?" Davis said.

"It's a job for an entire company or just one or two men," Dale said. "He robbed a bank in Grayson and killed the sheriff."

"He didn't come this way, I can tell you that," Davis said.

"I'm heading out right after we fill our stomach," Dale said. "Have you had lunch yet?"

"You look up to the mark," Davis said. He looked at Posey. "Especially you, big fellow. But Spooner is one nasty customer. Seems like he takes some kind of pleasure in killing."

"He does," Posey said, slicing into a steak.

Davis squinted at Posey. "You know him?"

"We served together under Sherman," Posey said. "I think that's where he got his taste for blood."

"How do you know he didn't travel east?" Dale asked.

"Railroad scouts protecting inventory," Davis said. "If his bunch came east, they would have spotted them."

"I figure we can make Grayson in three days and a bit if we leave this afternoon," Dale said. "We'll pick up enough supplies for the trip here and stock up there. Spooner's trail will be cold, but we have to start somewhere."

"We can save you two days of riding," Davis said. "We got track down three-quarters of the way to Alamosa for purpose of repairing busted cars and such. I can have a repair train take you out right after lunch."

"Our horses?" Dale asked.

"We'll hitch a boxcar," Davis said.

"As much as I was looking forward to sleeping on the hard ground, I'll take you up on your kind offer," Dale said.

"No thanks needed," Davis said. "The railroad wants that bastard as much as you do for all the trains he's robbed."

Dale and Posey rode with the engineer and coalman in the locomotive. The only other

61

car was the boxcar in tow that carried the horses.

Once they had rolled out of town and the engineer had the speed up to fifty miles an hour, he shouted, "Best get comfortable, gents. We got two hours of hard track in front of us."

"Up ahead is a loop where we turn around," the engineer said. "You fellows get off here, and good luck."

"Thanks for the ride," Dale said. "You saved us a lot of backaches."

Posey and Dale retrieved their horses from the boxcar and held them away from the track until the train had safely moved ahead and turned around. Once it had started back to Alamosa, Dale said, "We have six hours or so in the saddle to Grayson. We can ride for two hours until dark and get a fresh start in the morning or find a spot and camp here for the night. Which?"

Posey rubbed the large neck of his massive horse. "These boys have been sitting around for days. They need to run."

"Run it is," Dale said and got into the saddle.

After a light supper of bacon, beans, and cornbread and coffee, they rinsed and packed away the gear, opened the bedrolls, and settled in for the night. The hobbled horses nibbled on grass a few feet from the now extinguished campfire.

Posey rolled a cigarette, lit it, and looked up at the million stars covering the night sky.

"You have a good life, brother," Posey said. "Nice wife and kids, a home. How many more years are you going to break your back chasing outlaws?"

"Me and Sarah discussed it many times," Dale said. "In five years, I will have enough money socked away to return to the farm and start it up again. She can minister at the local church in town. My boy will be old enough by then to help with the work some after school."

"Pa was twenty-five or -six when he started the farm, and the work damn near killed him," Posey said. "You'll be what, forty-five? That's a hard age to take up such a rough life, Dale."

"Not if I hire a full-time man and grow potatoes," Dale said. "Potatoes will grow just about anywhere in any soil. Some hogs and horses on the side. It won't be so bad a life, Jack. Maybe I'll hire you."

"No, thanks," Posey said. "I had my share of busting rocks."

"If you had a good woman, a wife, maybe you'd feel different," Dale said.

"Maybe."

"All those years running around, hiding, working two-bit ranch jobs, you never came across a woman that struck your fancy?"

"The only thing that struck my fancy was keeping my neck out of a rope," Posey said.

"I'm asking you to think some on my offer, Jack," Dale said. "We'll be together again, and we can build a second house on the extra acres Pa never worked. There's a stream there, remember?"

"I remember, but it's all a lick and a promise if you ask me," Posey said.

"You're all balled up right now, I see that," Dale said. "When this business is finished, you'll feel different."

"Maybe," Posey said softly.

"Maybe nothing, Jack," Dale said. "It doesn't matter, your past. We're still brothers, and that can't be changed. Last year I hired an architect from Saint Louis to design a new farmhouse and barn. They start building it next spring. You could get a head start on me and go there until I retire. Remember, Jack, the farm is half yours. We split the crops, hogs, horses, everything right down the middle. How does that suit you, little brother?"

When Posey didn't answer, Dale rolled over and looked at his brother.

He was sound asleep.

CHAPTER SEVEN

Grayson was a small town that made its living mining minerals from the hills and mountains in Bryce Canyon.

A few hundred citizens, of which ninety percent worked digging minerals out of the ground. The sheriff had been only part-time, spending most of his time busting rock. The only reason the town even had the need of a sheriff was to protect the once-a-month payroll money, which was delivered by the mine owners from back east and locked up in the small safe at the bank.

Telegraph lines did run through the town out of necessity for the mining company.

On the delivery day, the sheriff deputized a few men as guards and a watch was set up overnight until the workers were paid the following day.

Shortly before dawn, Spooner and his men rode into Grayson and shot the two deputies standing watch in front of the bank. They kicked in the door of the bank and discovered the safe had a broken lock and, according to several witnesses, Spooner was laughing when he rode out of town after gunning down the half-dressed sheriff as he ran across the street, holding a shotgun.

According to the mining company, eight thousand seven hundred and fifty dollars in payroll cash was stolen.

"That was the report sent to me by the county sheriff," Dale said as he and Posey rode into the deserted streets of the small town.

"Sounds like Tom has grown even more bloody over the years," Posey said.

"The county sheriff is supposed to meet us here," Dale said. "Let's check the jail."

They dismounted and walked the horses along the wide, main boulevard that divided the tiny town in half.

Three horses were tethered to the post outside the building bearing a sign: *Town Jail and Sheriff's Office.*

Two county deputies sat in chairs, each with a tin mug of coffee and a shotgun.

"US Marshal Dale Posey," Dale said.

"Sheriff's expecting you," one of the deputies said.

"Any more of that coffee?" Posey said. "We rode all morning after a cold camp."

"Fresh pot," the deputy said.

Dale and Posey opened the door and entered the small office where the county sheriff sat behind a desk. A territorial map was spread out across the desk.

"US Marshal Dale Posey," Dale said.

"County Sheriff Sam Fey."

Posey walked to the small woodstove where a pot rested. "Okay?" he said.

"Help yourself," Fey said. "Cups are on the counter against the wall."

"We're going to try and pick up Spooner's tracks," Dale said. "Are you riding with us?"

"I am," Fey said. "I'm leaving my two men to guard the next payroll delivery."

Bringing two cups to the desk, Posey handed one to Dale and said, "Hell, Spooner's long gone."

"I know, but that murdering bastard may just be crafty enough to realize the payroll needs to be replaced and come back, figuring on another easy meal," Fey said.

"If that's the case, you and two men aren't enough to stop his bunch," Dale said.

"We armed the whole damn town," Fey said. "It will be like Jesse James riding into Northfield in 'seventy-six."

"Spooner's smart enough to know that," Posey said. "He'll stay free and clear for a while, hole up, and plan another job hell and gone from here."

Fey scrutinized Posey for a few seconds. "You talk like you know the man."

"We rode together under Sherman during the war," Posey said. "He's smarter than Jesse, Frank, and the Younger brothers combined. I'll bet he cut the telegraph lines so the town couldn't wire for help until they were repaired."

"He did," Fey admitted.

"I'd like to load up on supplies and fill our stomachs before we head out," Dale said. "Where can we do that in this town?"

Turned out that Grayson had a first-rate hotel and general store, both owned and operated by the mining company. When executives from back east traveled to check on mining operations, they needed a decent place to stay and had the hotel built. They invested in a good general store because they knew the townsfolk would spend their money in it, and the money would simply come back to them.

"I'd like to send a wire to my wife before we head out," Dale said.

"Lines are repaired," Fey said.

"Good," Dale said.

Posey looked around the dining hall in

the hotel lobby for the waitress. They had just finished a large lunch of steak, potatoes, and gravy and biscuits, and he wanted coffee before they left.

He caught her eyes and she came to the table.

"Coffee and . . . Dale, what was that cake you got me a week ago?" Posey said.

"Danish," Dale said.

"I've never heard of Danish," the waitress said. "What is it?"

"Sort of a cake," Posey said.

"We have excellent apple pie and peach pie made from canned fruit, but still very good," the waitress said.

"We take that two ways," Posey said.

"Which pie?" the waitress said.

"One of each," Posey said.

Dale led the way out of town following the northern route Spooner took as described by witnesses. Fey and Posey rode directly behind Dale. Each man's horse was loaded down with a week's worth of fresh supplies.

"Any townspeople follow this route since the robbery?" Dale asked.

"They mine northwest of town, so I'd guess not," Fey said.

"Jack," Dale said.

Posey nodded and rode ahead.

Fey looked at Dale.

"He used to scout for Sherman," Dale said.

Posey rode for several miles before picking up any signs of horses. It hadn't rained for weeks, and the land was dry enough for tracks to stay in the soft ground. They led toward the canyons no doubt.

Once they got to the rocks the trail would be difficult to follow.

From the saddle, Posey spotted something unusual and dismounted. He got low to the ground and inspected the tracks carefully. He put the number of horses at nine. Spooner and eight of his men.

One horse had a busted rear right shoe. Because of that, the horse's stride was off just a bit. Posey mounted up and kept close watch on the busted shoe, which made it a bit easier to follow.

He rode for several more miles, stopping to check every once in a while, keeping an eye on the busted shoe.

The horse was going lame. The busted shoe probably picked up a stone and was causing the horse a lot of discomfort, especially since they were still riding hard at this point.

Posey didn't have a pocket watch, but he

didn't need one. He knew by the placement of the sun in the sky how much daylight was left. There was about an hour, time to ride another mile or so before stopping to make camp.

Posey rode a half mile and stopped when he noticed the horse with the busted shoe was lagging behind.

He dismounted to check the tracks.

Spooner and the remaining seven riders didn't even bother to stop to check on the rider with the lame horse.

Posey walked his horse a bit, checking the tracks, and then decided on a spot to make camp. Come morning, the trail would be easy enough to pick up and follow.

He removed the saddle from his horse and immediately hobbled front and rear legs with leather strips. Then he gathered wood and built a campfire. He dug out the brush from a saddlebag and was brushing his horse when Dale and Fey arrived.

"No coffee?" Dale said.

"I got the sack of coffee, you got the pot," Posey said.

Supper was beans flavored with molasses, bacon, and hunks of cornbread, with coffee to wash it all down with.

"I can't say for sure at this point if they're

headed directly to the canyons, but Spooner's definitely riding to higher ground," Posey said.

"Without any law pursuing him, I wouldn't be surprised if they holed up in those canyons for a while," Fey said.

"I doubt it," Posey said.

They were seated around the crackling campfire and flickering light reflected off Posey's face.

"Why do you say that?" Fey asked.

"I studied the recent jobs he pulled," Posey said. "Every two weeks he strikes. I believe he has a centralized hideout that's never more than two weeks' ride in any direction. He might hole up in the canyons for a day or two to rest the horses, but he won't stay. These canyons aren't centralized to the robberies he's pulled."

"Why didn't you say that earlier?" Dale asked.

"I figured you saw that on your own," Posey said.

"Then what's the point of following these tracks to a place he no longer is?" Fey asked.

"See which direction he took afterward," Posey said. "It might give us an idea where he's headed next."

"My jurisdiction ends at the county line," Fey said.

"Correct me if I am wrong, Dale, but can't you temporarily deputize a man a deputy marshal if need be?" Posey said.

"I can," Dale said. "If need be."

Fey sighed. "Swear me in when we reach the county line," he said.

Posey, finished with supper, rolled a cigarette. "I'll get an early start in the morning. Follow my tracks until noon. What kind of game they have in these parts?"

"Usual. Mule deer, wild turkey, rabbit," Fey said.

"I'll see if I can spot something worth shooting," Posey said. "Beans and bacon gets pretty old after a while."

"Grown particular the past week?" Dale said.

Grinning, Posey said, "The past two years. Night, gents."

CHAPTER EIGHT

Posey watched the tiny black dots in the sky fly in a circular pattern. They were a good eight hours away, close to the entrance of the canyons or even in them. Every so often the dots would land and others would take their place in the sky.

The dots were buzzards feasting on the carcass of a dead animal. Dale had the good sense to pack binoculars in the saddlebags, and he dug out his pair and scanned the buzzards.

He counted eleven circling in the sky, with probably the like number on the ground.

The carcass was large. Large enough to feed an army of those filthy birds.

Posey went to the fire where he had two hares roasting on a spit, a fry pan of beans, and the coffee pot keeping warm. He turned the hares and then sat to wait for Dale and Fey.

They arrived as he removed the hares

from the fire and set them on his tin plate to cool next to the beans.

"Could smell that a mile downwind," Dale said as he dismounted.

"Buzzards," Fey said, looking at the sky.

"We won't make them tonight," Posey said. "We'll have to wait until morning to see what the filthy beasts are eating."

"Maybe a deer or dead bear?" Fey said.

"Lame horse," Posey said. "I've been tracking it since yesterday. He couldn't keep up with Spooner and the rest."

"Left him behind?" Fey asked.

"The horse, at least," Posey said. "Won't know about the rider until we reach the carcass."

"Spooner won't care about one man left behind," Dale said.

"Probably not," Posey said. "Let's eat."

Posey rode well ahead the rest of the afternoon and made camp two hours' ride from the site of the carcass. The buzzards were still circling, which meant there was still plenty of meat left on the dead horse's bones.

Buzzards ate anything so long as it was dead. They could eat week-old, rotting flesh, man or beast, and never get sick. They always seemed to go for the eyes first. Posey had witnessed that firsthand when he was scouting for Sherman and came across a band of dead Confederate soldiers rotting in the sun.

The buzzards were pecking out the eyes first and squabbling with each other over who got to eat first.

He was armed with an eighteen-sixty Navy Colt pistol and Henry rifle and used both to kill as many of the buzzards as possible. Since that time, Posey disliked even the sight of the scavenging birds.

Earlier he heard Dale's Winchester fire one shot, and Posey knew that he would arrive with supper soon. He built a campfire, put on a pot of coffee, and gave the horse a good brushing.

Dale and Fey arrived right around sunset. Dale had a small wild turkey hanging off his saddle.

"I see you brought groceries," Posey said as Dale dismounted, holding the bird.

"Tomorrow we ride to the canyons together," Posey said. "Check out the dead horse and try to pick up Spooner's trail."

"And if we can't find a trail?" Fey asked.

"Everybody leaves a trail," Posey said. "Dead or alive."

CHAPTER NINE

Posey dismounted a hundred or so feet from the dead horse the buzzards were feasting on. They had eaten several hundred pounds off its decomposing flesh. He placed the bandanna around his neck over his mouth and nose so he could go in for a closer look.

Behind him Fey said, "The stench."

"I smelled worse," Posey said as he closed to within fifty feet of the dead horse.

The buzzards reacted to him being so close. Some squawked at him, others hopped away and took flight.

The rider had taken his saddle and walked away northeast toward the canyons. Spooner and the others didn't wait for him according to the tale of the tracks.

"Jack?" Dale said still atop his horse.

Posey turned and walked to his horse and mounted up. "Spooner left the man behind to walk."

"Walk to where?" Fey asked.

"Let's find out," Posey said.

Posey followed the footprints of the man walking as he followed the tracks of Spooner and his men. At the pass leading into the canyons, Posey, Dale, and Fey paused on horseback and looked at the looming rocks, peaks, and canyon walls as they glowed a bright crimson color in the afternoon sun.

"A man could get lost in there," Dale said.

"They probably took this path in and found another out at some point," Posey said. "Keep your eyes open for tracks and signs."

They rode for a while, and then Posey dismounted to check for signs.

Spooner made no effort at all to hide his tracks. He knew no one had followed him from Grayson and no one knew his destination, so why bother?

Posey returned to his horse and mounted up. "We can ride until dark and eat in the saddle for lunch," he said. "I'd like to see where these tracks lead to."

"We got cornbread and corn dodgers, enough for several days," Dale said.

"Pass 'em around," Posey said.

Several miles deep into the canyons, Posey suddenly stopped his horse.

"What?" Fey said behind Posey. "What is it?"

Posey ignored the question and looked up at the canyon walls. The passing sun had changed their color to a dull red. He remembered a story he read in a newspaper a few years ago about the planet Mars. Scientists with powerful telescopes claimed the surface of the planet was red, and they were speculating as to the reasons why.

Maybe it was something as simple as the shifting sunlight.

"Jack?" Dale said softly from behind Posey.

Posey held his right hand up as a sign for Dale and Fey to keep quiet. Posey kept his eyes glued to the canyon walls near the top. Some time passed. Seconds, minutes, he wasn't sure.

Then a pebble slid down the canyon wall to the right.

"Ambush!" Posey yelled as the first shot rang out and hit Fey in the chest.

As Fey toppled from his horse, a second shot hit Dale in the upper right leg. The horse reared up in fear and Dale fell from the saddle.

Posey jumped from the saddle and ran to Dale.

"Jack, I . . ." Dale said.

"Quiet," Posey said and grabbed Dale and dragged him close to the right canyon wall.

Once against the wall, Posey looked at Dale's leg.

"How bad?" Dale asked.

"Bad," Posey said.

"Jack, how did . . . ?" Dale said.

"Quiet," Posey said. "We got to stop the bleeding."

Posey removed Dale's holster and set it aside, then opened and removed Dale's belt and bandanna from around his neck. He tied the bandanna around Dale's right leg, then used the belt as a tourniquet to stop the bleeding.

"Now just hold still," Posey said.

"Fey?" Dale asked.

Posey looked at Fey and shook his head.

"Aw, Jesus," Dale said.

"You down there," a man on the top of the canyon wall shouted. "I want no more killing. I just want your horse. That's all. Ride out and leave one horse and there'll be no more shooting."

"The second we move to a horse he'll kill us both," Dale whispered.

"Stay against the wall," Posey whispered. "He can't see us against the wall."

"We can't just sit here, Jack," Dale said.

"I know. When you see me start to climb,

81

start talking to him," Posey said.

"Climb the . . . ?" Dale said.

Hugging the wall, Posey turned and ran about a hundred feet behind where the man stood on the canyon cliff, then looked back and nodded.

"Hey, you in the cliff," Dale shouted.

Posey started to climb the sixty or so feet to the top of the cliff.

"I'm listening," the man shouted.

"You killed my partner and the other is unconscious," Dale yelled. "I can't ride out and leave him to die."

"Put him on a horse then," the man shouted. "I only need one horse and some supplies."

"Too thin," Dale shouted. "I need some assurances."

He looked at Posey, and he was halfway up the cliff.

"Assurances like what?" the man shouted.

"Like you won't kill us," Dale shouted.

"I told you, I only need one horse," the man shouted.

"What about our supplies and money?" Dale shouted.

"Mister, I'm running out of patience with you," the man shouted. "Do as I say or I'll topple half this cliff down on you and take what I want over your dead body."

Dale looked up at Posey. He was at the top and cautiously making his way onto the cliff.

"Well, which horse do you want?" Dale shouted.

"Leave me the dead man's," the man shouted. "He ain't needing it no more."

"All right, I'll leave you the dead man's horse," Dale shouted. "You aren't going to shoot."

"I said I won't shoot," the man shouted.

Posey was on his feet and walking to the man, who was on his hands and knees, looking down. He had a rifle by his side.

"You won't shoot?" Dale shouted.

"Are you deef? I said I won't shoot," the man said. "Get on with it already 'fore I change my mind."

Posey was fifty feet from the man when the man looked to his left and saw Posey and jumped to his knees. He made a grab for his rifle and Posey drew his black Colt, cocked, fired, and shot the man in the chest.

The man fell over backward and sprawled out, but held onto the rifle. Posey rushed to the man's side as the man tried to cock the lever and Posey stepped on the man's arm.

"Ya kilt me," the man said.

Posey kicked the rifle away.

"You ride with Tom Spooner," Posey said.

"Ya kilt me for sure," the man said.

"You're not killed, not yet," Posey said. "Tell me where Spooner hides out and I'll let you live."

"I'm kilt, damn you," the man said.

"Where did Spooner go?" Posey said. "Where are you supposed to meet him?"

"Why should I tell anything to a man what kilt me?" the man said.

"Because I'll let you live if you do."

"Give me a hand up and stop the bleeding and I'll tell ya," the man said.

Posey holstered his Colt and extended his right hand to the man. The man took Posey's hand and as Posey lifted him, the man aimed the derringer hidden in his left hand at Posey.

Posey released the man's hand and he fell backward just as the shot fired into the air above Posey's head.

"That wasn't very smart," Posey said.

"You go to hell," the man said.

"Where is Tom Spooner?" Posey asked.

"I'm kilt," the man said and closed his eyes.

"Damn," Posey said.

Down below, Dale yelled, "Jack, are you all right?"

"Yeah. I'm coming down," Posey said.

■ ■ ■ ■

Posey used Fey's canteen to wash the blood away from the bullet hole in Dale's right leg and then poured whiskey from the bottle Sarah gave them onto the wound.

"I can't get that bullet out," Posey said. "It's a .44 Winchester slug. Where is the nearest town?"

"Go back out of the canyon and ride northeast," Dale said. "Maybe twenty miles is a tiny town called Cannonville. I stopped there once before about a year ago. They don't have a doctor, but they have a barber who studied medicine a few years back east."

"Okay," Posey said.

Posey used his bandanna to wrap Dale's leg, then Dale's belt to tie it tight to slow the bleeding.

"I'm going to tie your hands to the saddle horn and your legs to the stirrups, so if you feel like passing out, go ahead," Posey said.

Posey, with Dale's horse in tow, raced across the flats of Utah toward Cannonville. There were about ninety minutes of daylight left, and he needed to reach the town before dark. If he didn't and they got lost, there was the risk of rot to Dale's leg, and he could lose it.

Fortunately, Dale had the good sense to keep large and powerful horses on hand, and they had little trouble keeping the pace Posey demanded.

He glanced back once or twice, and Dale had passed out in the saddle.

Posey glanced at the sun. Thirty minutes of light left and at least three more miles.

He dug in and yanked the reins hard. "Come on, you beast, work for your supper," he said.

Sweat formed on the horses' legs and chest and as they flared their nostrils and ran harder, sheets of sweat flew off their bodies.

A few minutes before sundown, the tiny town of Cannonville appeared a few hundred yards ahead, and Posey slowed the horses to a fast gait and then a quickstep so they could cool off slowly.

"Let's walk in with some dignity," he told his horse.

CHAPTER TEN

The barber's name was Jed Melville, and if he cut hair with half the skill he removed the bullet from Dale's leg, a man would look like a back east dandy for sure.

Posey and Melville's wife assisted him with removing the bullet, although all Posey did was hold Dale still while Melville cut and stitched. Melville's wife held a candle for light and wiped away blood with a wet cloth.

Afterward, Melville's wife, a short woman named Sally, served tea in the parlor of their home next door to the barbershop where Dale rested in a bed.

"It isn't every day a US marshal shows up on my doorstep with a bullet in him," Melville said. "What happened?"

Posey tasted the tea. It was god-awful stuff, but he didn't want to be impolite, so he drank it while he told Melville what happened.

"He's a vile, evil man," Sally said.

"You know him?" Posey asked.

"He and his bunch rode through here about six months ago looking for supplies," Melville said. "We have no law except a county sheriff, and he's a day's ride from here. He paid for what they needed and went on his way, which surprised the hell out of me."

"This town is so small, how does it exist out here by itself?" Posey asked.

"Surrounding this town in a circle is about thirty ranches and farms, and they get most of what they need from us," Melville said. "If this dot on the map weren't here, most of them ranchers and farmers would have a day's ride there and back for supplies."

"So Spooner knew this town had a good supply store?" Posey asked.

"I guess. I don't know. Is that important?" Melville asked.

"Not really," Posey said. "Is the marshal going to recover?"

"Be about a week before he's fit to travel," Melville said. "He lost a lot of blood, but he's a fit, strong man."

"I meant return to his duties."

"A month, six weeks," Melville said. "He goes bouncing around before that, and he's liable to open that wound, and it's a deep one. It's lucky you got here when you did. That leg could have gone rotten on him."

"How long before he wakes up?" Posey asked.

"I wouldn't bother him until morning," Melville said.

"We have an extra room for you to sleep in," Sally said. "You must be hungry. Finish your tea, and I'll fix you something to eat."

"I wouldn't want to put you out," Posey said.

"Nonsense. Jed, go check on the marshal while I fix some food," Sally said.

Posey lowered his knife and fork and looked at Sally. "That was the best steak I've had in a decade, ma'am," he said.

"Thank you, young man," Sally said. "Would you care for another glass of buttermilk?"

"I couldn't put one more thing in my stomach," Posey said.

The back door to the kitchen opened and, holding a lantern, Melville returned.

"Well, he'll sleep until morning," Melville said. "Then I'll check the wound. He might have a fever set in overnight."

"A fever. Why?" Posey asked.

"Body's natural reaction to infection."

"What was that stuff you used to put him

to sleep?" Posey asked.

"It's called chloroform," Melville said.

"I'll go sit with him for a while," Sally said. "If he takes on a fever, I'll come get you."

After Sally left the kitchen, Melville asked, "Would you care to join me for a sip of bourbon whiskey on the porch?"

"There's still a bit of a chill to the night air in these parts," Melville said.

Posey took a sip of bourbon whiskey, and then rolled a cigarette.

"The marshal will be wanting to pay you for your services," Posey said.

"Two kinds of people I never charge," Melville said. "Lawmen and Indians in need."

"I can't speak for Indians, but Dale Posey can be one right stubborn man," Posey said. "He'll insist on paying his way."

"And speaking on him, I best go have a look," Melville said. "Feel free to have another shot of bourbon if you desire."

After Melville left the porch, Posey filled his shot glass and took a small sip.

He looked at the stars in the Utah sky. They twinkled silently in the darkness.

He took another small sip of bourbon.

Tomorrow morning, once he made sure

Dale was all right, he would get on that big horse and simply ride away. Make a quick stop at the farm and then head west to California or Oregon, change his name, and lose himself in a sea of pilgrims seeking new lives and forgetting old ones.

Dale would recover and in a month or six weeks, he'd start out after Spooner again, only he wouldn't catch him. Dale was a good, honest lawman, and to catch Tom Spooner required someone just as crafty, dangerous, and dishonest as Spooner himself.

Posey took another sip of bourbon and then sighed. Dale was a good man, and he was not. That was a hard fact, but true nonetheless.

Men have to be what they are and not what someone else wants them to be. Dale was a lawman, husband, father, and good man in his soul.

Posey was everything his brother wasn't.

How he got that way was not important.

Come morning, he'd be gone and that was important.

Everything else was just a bunch of in-betweens.

CHAPTER ELEVEN

A knock on the bedroom door woke Posey and when he opened his eyes, it was still dark outside the open window beside the bed.

"It's Sally," Melville's wife said. "My husband needs your assistance. The marshal has a fever."

Wearing his shirt open, Posey looked at his brother.

"I figured fever would set in, and it has," Melville said.

"What can you do?" Posey asked.

"Help me carry him to that bathtub in the corner," Melville said. "After that, Sally will take you to the icehouse. I'll need you to chop enough ice to fill the tub."

"How much is enough?" Posey asked.

"At least a wheelbarrow full," Melville said. "Now hurry."

The icehouse was basically a small barn without windows. Hay lined the floor and bales of it lined the walls. Blocks of ice were stacked in the center, each wrapped in burlap.

There was a chopping block, ice picks, and axes, and Posey had to chop three blocks of ice to fill a wheelbarrow for the bathtub.

Once Dale was packed in ice, his unconscious body began to shiver and sweat at the same time.

Melville and Sally had stripped Dale down to his bare skin and wrapped a towel around his waist; otherwise he was naked in the freezing cold tub.

Posey had seen army doctors use ice to bring down the fever of wounded soldiers during the war. Sometimes the soldiers lived and sometimes they didn't.

Sally felt Dale's face. "It's working," she said.

"Give him five more minutes and then help me carry him to the bed," Melville said.

Once Dale was in bed and covered with sheets and blankets, Sally went to prepare breakfast.

Melville checked Dale's fever after he had stopped shivering.

"It's down, but not all the way," he said. "Let him warm up a bit, and it's back in the tub."

After another fifteen minutes in the tub of ice, Melville was satisfied that Dale's fever had broken.

They returned him to bed and covered him in sheets and blankets and then went to the kitchen where Sally had breakfast waiting.

"You men eat, and I'll sit with the marshal," Sally said.

The table was set with scrambled eggs, bacon, potatoes, toast, and coffee.

"After his fever doesn't return, he'll wake up and he'll be hungry as a bear," Melville said.

"What happened?" Dale asked. "I don't remember a thing after you put me on my horse."

"That's because you passed out," Posey said.

"Eat," Sally said. "Talk later."

Dale nodded and dug into the plate of scrambled eggs, bacon, and potatoes.

Posey had a cup of coffee and sat in the chair opposite the bed.

"I'll be back after you've had the chance to eat," Melville said.

"And if you want more, let me know," Sally said.

"I will, thank you," Dale said.

After Melville and Sally left the bedroom, Posey rolled a cigarette.

"How long was I out?" Dale asked.

"Close to two days."

"You been here the whole time?"

"Somebody had to be around to stick you in ice."

"Ice? I had a fever?"

Posey nodded as he struck a match. "Mr. Melville saved your life and your leg."

"I know and I'll thank him properly," Dale said. "But right now I need you to do something for me."

Posey sipped some coffee and looked at Dale.

"Ask Mr. Melville where the nearest telegraph station is," Dale said. "I'll write out what I want you to send if you get me paper and pencil."

"It's probably a two-day ride to the nearest town with a telegraph office," Posey said. "Can't it wait?"

"There's a murdered sheriff we left back there," Dale said. "We owe him the respect of having someone claim the body. Sarah needs to know what happened and that I'm alive. I'll probably be in bed for a while healing, so I'll have my deputies come get me by wagon. You and two of my deputies can continue the search until I'm back on my feet again."

"Dale, you said it yourself, this is a job for a whole company or one or two men," Posey said. "I'm not teaming up with some of your pip-squeak deputies. Not to hunt down Tom Spooner and his bunch. They'll only get killed."

"Jack, ride to the telegraph office and send the wires for me," Dale said. "We'll talk about the rest when you get back."

Posey sighed. "All right, brother," he said.

"No need to ride all the way back to Grayson," Melville said. "A day's ride from here east is a railroad water stop. They have a telegraph set up for emergency use. Can you climb a pole?"

Dale folded the sheets of paper and handed them to Posey.

"One more thing," Dale said. "Hand me my saddlebags."

Posey tucked the folded sheets of paper into his shirt pocket and then lifted Dale's saddlebags off the floor and placed them behind the bed.

"Now raise your right hand," Dale said.

"What?"

"Your right hand, raise it," Dale said.

Slowly, Posey held up his right hand.

"Do you swear to uphold the . . ."

"No, no, no, don't do this to me, Dale," Posey said.

"Do you swear to uphold the law as a duly appointed United States Deputy Marshal," Dale said.

"You son of a bitch," Posey said.

"Swear it," Dale said. "For once in your miserable life, you're going to do the right thing."

Posey sighed as he looked at Dale.

"I swear," Posey said.

Dale dug into one of the saddlebags and then tossed Posey a US deputy marshal's badge.

"Put this on," Dale said.

Posey looked at the badge in his hand.

"I think I'd rather be back in Yuma," he said.

"I can arrange that if you prefer," Dale said. "Now get going."

CHAPTER TWELVE

Posey rode east in the direction of the railroad water stop. Melville said he should reach the site by late afternoon. He figured that after sending the telegrams, he would just keep on going and reach Grand Junction by the following morning.

It was a damned fool thing Dale did, pinning a badge on him. When he didn't return, he would see just how foolish an idea it was.

Being a lawman was a ridiculous notion for sure.

The truth was, Posey deserved to be in Yuma and he knew it. He did commit many of the crimes with Spooner that he was accused of, except that he wasn't the killer Spooner was.

Tom Spooner had cold, almost lifeless gray eyes that never appeared real when he looked at you. When Posey was a kid, his father bought him a bag of marbles. It was a game popular in Europe at the time. The smooth, round balls of glass reminded Posey of Spooner's eyes.

Beautiful, but lifeless, like the eyes of a rattlesnake.

He reached the railroad tracks. Millville said when he reached the tracks to follow them east for about an hour.

Posey dismounted and rolled a cigarette and sat on a railroad tie to smoke it. The horse wandered a few feet away and grazed on some grass.

He would have been better off letting Dale's leg rot. Maybe he'd be a cripple, but at least he'd be alive. Once he recovered and set out after Spooner again, his chances of living were reduced greatly.

"Damn you, Dale," Posey said aloud.

The horse looked at him.

"What?" Posey said. "Eat your grass, you stupid beast."

The water stop was like hundreds of others across the country. A giant water tank adjacent to the tracks, a large pile of chopped wood and coal, and a cabin set back about fifty feet where workers slept.

It was close to five in the afternoon and smoke gently billowed from the chimney in the cabin when Posey arrived.

A railroad man was chopping wood at the pile. Another came out of the cabin and stood on the porch. He held a shotgun.

"No need for that scattergun, mister," Posey said. "I just need to send a few telegrams, is all."

"Our wire is for federal use only," the man chopping wood said.

Posey moved his vest out of the way to expose the deputy marshal's badge.

"Come on down," the man on the porch said. "Have some supper with us, Marshal. We'll send your wires after we eat."

Supper was beef stew with potatoes and carrots cooked in a large iron pot over a fire in the fireplace and bread.

Furnishings were simple. Three beds, a table with chairs, a cabinet for dishes, an indoor pump for water, a small woodstove, and a cabinet for rifles.

"I'm Wallace," the man who had been chopping wood said. "This here is Tubbs, my partner."

Wiping sauce off his plate with bread, Tubbs nodded.

"So what telegrams do you need to send?" Wallace asked.

Posey removed the folded papers from his pocket and set them on the table. Wallace picked up the papers and read them carefully.

"He's a bad one, that Tom Spooner," Wallace said. "Him and his bunch."

"Spooner, that son of a bitch," Tubbs said.

"You know him?" Posey asked.

"He robbed three trains along the Northern Pacific in the last two years," Tubbs said. "Killed two engineers and one conductor."

"He deserves to swing at the end of a rope, that one," Wallace said. "Him and his entire bunch."

"Well, if you want to send them wires, let's get to it," Tubbs said.

Posey looked up at the twenty-five-foot-high telegraph pole. He wore a lumberjack's spikes on his boots and a harness around his waist that encircled the pole.

"Why is the telegraph machine way up there on a hook?" Posey said.

"So nobody can get to it when we ain't around," Wallace said.

"Now scoot up there and bring it down," Tubbs said.

"I've never climbed a pole before," Posey said.

"Nothing to it," Tubbs said. "Use them spurs and climb up like a monkey."

Posey dug the spur on his left boot into

the wood pole, then the right. Using the harness, he shimmied up the pole several feet. He repeated the process a dozen times or more until he was able to lift the telegraph off its hook.

"Untangle the wire and lower it down to us, but be careful not to get a shock," Tubbs said. "When it's all the way down, drape that metal hook over the lines."

Slowly, Posey lowered the telegraph to the ground where Tubbs caught it.

"Now place that hook over the wires," Wallace said. "And . . ."

Posey placed the hook over the wires and sparks flew everywhere. He yanked his hand back and looked down.

"Watch out for the sparks," Wallace said.

"Thanks," Posey said.

Tubbs set the telegraph on a small table they brought out from the cabin.

"Okay, Marshal, come down and we'll do this," Tubbs said.

Posey slowly lowered himself to the ground, and when he reached bottom, he said, "That's a bit tiresome. How do you gents do it?"

"We got a thirty-foot ladder around back," Wallace said. "We use that."

"Where's that chair?" Tubbs asked.

■ ■ ■ ■

Posey took a sip of coffee as he stood next to Wallace in the dark. An oil lantern on the table provided enough light for Tubbs to see and write the reply when it came.

"How long you boys been working for the railroad?" Posey asked.

"Since 'sixty-seven," Tubbs said.

"About the same," Wallace said. "Want me to sweeten that?"

Posey held his cup out and Wallace added an ounce of rye to it from a pint bottle.

"We was telegraph operators for the Union Army during the war," Tubbs said. "We went to work for the railroad right after."

"You don't live here in this cabin?" Posey asked.

"I got a small spread about five miles to the north," Tubbs said. "A missus and five young'ens."

"My place is about three miles east," Wallace said. "My missus and three boys watch the place while I'm here."

"We work a week on and a week off," Tubbs said. "Another crew comes in when we go home."

"How often does a train come by?" Posey asked.

"Well, let's see now," Wallace said. "We got the ten a.m. east, the noon west, the two p.m. east, and the four p.m. west, and then nothing until the midnight west."

The telegraph suddenly jumped to life with a few taps on the keypad.

Tubbs tapped his response and took the pencil from his pocket. When the message came, he wrote each word on a piece of paper. Finished, he tapped a sign off and then handed the paper to Posey.

"That one is from the marshal's office in Santa Fe," Tubbs said. "Still waiting on a reply from that county sheriff's office."

"My missus brought out an apple pie this morning," Wallace said. "Why don't I get us each a slice and some fresh coffee?"

The response from the county sheriff's office came an hour later. Tubbs copied the message, signed off, and gave the paper to Posey.

"Well, let's grab some sleep before the midnight train arrives," Wallace said.

The entire cabin seemed to rattle as the midnight train rolled to a stop at the water tank.

Posey opened his eyes as Tubbs and Wallace were putting their boots on. He sat up in the bed and grabbed his boots.

Tubbs and Wallace were at the train by the time he stepped out onto the porch. He rolled a cigarette, lit it with a wood match, and smoked as he watched them service the train.

Wallace worked the spout and lowered it to the water tank on the train. Tubbs loaded wood onto the locomotive. The entire procedure took but ten minutes, and the train was on its way.

Walking on to the porch, Wallace said, "Well, that's it until morning. Best get some sleep."

After washing up at the pump and eating breakfast with Wallace and Tubbs, Posey was on his way.

He rode southwest until he was out of sight of the cabin, and then turned north. He rode for several miles before he brought the horse to a stop.

"Serves you right, Dale," Posey said aloud. "Nobody told you to go pin a badge on me. I ain't trustworthy. That's why I was in prison. You ought to know that."

He gave the reins a tug and the horse moved forward. After about a minute, Posey yanked the reins and the horse stopped. He slid out of the saddle and walked twenty feet or so away from the horse.

"Damn you all to hell," Posey shouted. "This is what you get when you trust an outlaw."

He picked up a rock at his feet and threw it against a tree.

And screamed so loud, it startled the horse.

Then he rushed back to the horse and mounted the saddle in one quick swoop.

"Come on," Posey said as he turned the horse south.

Posey arrived in Cannonville in time to have supper with Melville and his wife, Sally.

Pan-fried chicken with gravy, biscuits and potatoes, and peach pie for dessert, although, as Sally apologized for, the peaches came from a can.

"I took him his supper right before you arrived," Sally said. "He's doing much better. I expect he'll be able to travel within a week."

"I best go see him," Posey said after supper.

"Take him a piece of pie and a glass of buttermilk and another slice for yourself," Sally said.

"Let me see the responses," Dale said as he sliced into the peach pie.

Posey removed the folded papers from his shirt pocket and handed them to Dale.

Dale read them both as he finished his pie.

"When we get home to Santa Fe, I figure I should be fit to travel in a month," Dale said. "By then, Spooner probably will have struck again, and we'll have a fresh trail."

"A month?" Posey said.

"I can't do hard riding until this leg is properly healed."

"And I do what, sit around and watch your leg scab over for a month?"

"What are you saying, Jack?"

Posey sighed as he dug out his pouch and papers and rolled a cigarette. As he struck a match, he said, "You won't find or catch Tom Spooner, Dale. And if you did, he'd kill you for sure. That's what I'm saying."

"A lawman doesn't pick and choose who to go after and when to enforce the law, Jack. As long as I wear this badge, I will carry out my duties."

"Even if it makes Sarah a widow and your kids orphans?" Posey asked.

"Orphans have no parents, Jack. They'd be fatherless, not orphans."

"Look, I know you're game, but game don't mean a thing to the likes of Spooner," Posey said. "And I know what orphan means. All I'm saying is I'm going at this alone. You said yourself this is a job for an entire company or one or two men."

"What do you mean, alone?" Dale asked.

"First thing tomorrow morning, I'm heading out after Spooner," Posey said.

"You can't do that," Dale said.

"From where I stand, Dale, you're in no position to stop me," Posey said.

"But why?" Dale asked. "Spooner's been on the loose for more than a decade. What's another month?"

"My mind's made up, Dale," Posey said. "You got me pardoned to help you catch Tom Spooner, and that's what I'm going to do."

"Alone," Dale said. "You'll just get yourself killed."

"Better me than you," Posey said. "I'll see you before I ride out."

After Posey left the room, Dale sighed and said, "Damn fool."

"Get your dirty clothes together, and I'll have them clean by morning," Sally said.

"That's very kind of you," Posey said.

"You'll need supplies," Melville said. "The store usually opens at nine, but I can have them open at eight so you can get what you need."

"I appreciate it, both of you," Posey said.

"I'm going to talk to Bart about opening the store early for you," Melville said. "I won't be long."

After Melville left the kitchen, Sally said, "More coffee? Jed told me how much you dislike tea."

"I would, thank you," Posey said.

Sally stood up from the table to fetch the pot from the woodstove and filled Posey's cup. After she returned the pot, she sat and looked at him.

"What's gnawing at you that you'd risk your life going after a bunch like Spooner's on your own?" she asked.

Posey took a sip from his cup but didn't answer.

"Oh, I've seen that look before," Sally said. "When we first came out here in 'fifty-one with a settlement and after the war when men were desperate. I suppose it's none of my business, so you pay me no never mind."

Posey stared up at the dark ceiling above his head and knew sleep wouldn't be arriving anytime soon tonight.

Something he didn't tell Dale, or anyone else for that matter. He never believed that story the Pinkerton detectives told him about the ranch foreman recognizing his black Colt Peacemaker.

For one thing, Posey rarely wore that Colt while working on a ranch. He wore an old, dented, nickel-plated Smith & Wesson .44 and kept the Colt in his saddlebags. The other thing that always bothered him was how the man who turned him in was mysteriously killed six months later.

He suspected Spooner was behind the whole thing. Maybe because he didn't fancy the notion of Posey roaming free with the knowledge of his crimes, and using the ranch foreman was an easy and convenient way of getting rid of him.

Killing the ranch foreman served two purposes. Get rid of the witness and pick up what was left of the reward money.

In all the years Posey was separated from Spooner, he never breathed a word about the man to anybody. Even when those six Pinkerton men rode up armed with shotguns to arrest him when he was unarmed and branding cows for the Big Whiskey Ranch, he never said a word.

Before his trial, when the federal prosecutor wanted to make a deal for Spooner in exchange for a reduced sentence, Posey kept his mouth shut and took his medicine.

So maybe a bit of Posey's desire to hunt

down Spooner was revenge. Who could blame him?

What did the law care so long as the job got done?

That's what Posey told himself just before sleep finally came.

Chapter Thirteen

"The shopkeeper said to give you this voucher for my supplies," Posey said and handed the paper to Dale.

"Forty-seven dollars? What did you buy?" Dale asked.

"Plates, coffee pot, food supplies, and ammunition," Posey said. "It was the ammunition that jacked up the bill."

Dale looked at the long trail knife hanging off the left side of Posey's gun belt. "How much for that Bowie?"

"Four dollars and worth every penny," Posey said.

Dale sighed. "I can't stop you, Jack," he said. "But I can ask you not to do anything to disgrace that badge I pinned on your shirt."

"Want it back?" Posey asked.

"No."

"Take care of Sarah and the kids," Posey said.

"Jack, wait," Dale said.

Posey looked at Dale.

"Where are you going?"

"Montana."

The best the railroad could do was take Posey to Miles City in Montana, and even that took two days because of all the stops and changes along the way. It was four o'clock in the afternoon when it finally did arrive, too late in the day to ride and too early in the day for sleep.

Posey walked his horse off the boxcar to the street where he paused and looked around. Soldiers were everywhere: walking the streets, in wagons, on the wood plank sidewalks.

It wasn't unusual to see soldiers in Miles City, as the army established two forts nearby after the Battle of Little Bighorn in 'seventy-six.

Posey walked his horse to a wide livery stable at the edge of town. A hunched-over manager greeted him at the corral.

"Overnight and give him your best grain," Posey said.

"Two dollars," the manager said. "In advance."

Posey took the Sharps and Winchester rifles and saddlebags with him when he left the livery and walked into town. Besides the usual array of shops, stores, gunsmiths, and blacksmiths, there was an unusually high number of saloons and gambling houses. Almost every saloon and gambling house had a brothel on the second floor.

The last time Posey passed through Miles City, it had a population of around three hundred. It had doubled since then, mostly because of the army.

As he walked the streets, some glanced his way, seeing the badge on his chest, looking at it with mild curiosity.

At the end of Miles Street sat a large jail and the city marshal's office. Posey opened the office door and stepped inside. There were three wood desks, one of which was occupied by a baby-faced deputy.

"Marshal," the deputy said as he stood up.

"You got a city marshal named Carver and a town sheriff named Smalls?" Posey asked.

"Yes sir, Marshal," the deputy said.

"Where are they?" Posey asked.

"This time a day they'd be over to the Last Chance Saloon," the deputy said. "They own it, you see."

"I'm going to leave my long guns and saddlebags here," Posey said. "I'll be back for them later."

Posey found the Last Chance Saloon a few blocks away on Main Street. It was a large saloon, with several different types of gambling tables, including roulette and faros, a long, mirrored bar, and a second-floor brothel. A piano in the corner was manned by an old-timer who played out of tune.

Every table and spot at the bar was occupied, but Posey had little trouble spotting Carver and Smalls as they stood behind the roulette wheel.

Bar girls were everywhere, serving drinks to soldiers and cowboys, enticing them to the second-floor brothel.

Posey merged through the crowd and elbowed his way to the bar. One of two bartenders on duty approached him.

"Give me a shot of your best bourbon and send one each to the marshal and sheriff over there behind the roulette wheel," Posey said. "And have your prettiest girl deliver it."

The bartender looked at the badge on Posey's chest and nodded.

Posey rolled a cigarette, lit it, and watched in the mirror as a saloon girl delivered the drinks to Carver and Smalls. As they took the shots, the girl pointed to the bar. The crowd parted for Carver and Smalls as if

Moses himself walked to the bar. Just before Carver touched Posey on the back, Posey spun around and looked at them.

"Howdy, boys," Posey said. "I see you prospered since we parted ways."

Shock registered on the faces of Carver and Smalls.

"Jesus Christ," Carver said.

"Well I'll be damned," Smalls said.

"What's it been, eight years?" Carver said.

"At least," Posey said.

"We heard you did a stretch in Yuma," Smalls said.

"Arrested on a false technicality they called it," Posey said. "Got a full pardon."

Carver looked at the badge on Posey's chest. "That for real, Jack?"

"It is," Posey said. "You got a place where we can talk private?"

There was a large office on the second floor behind the brothel. Posey sat at the table with Carver and Smalls. Carver poured three drinks from a decanter and said, "This is the good stuff, Jack. Come all the way from Kentucky."

Smalls opened a cigar box on the table and removed three.

"Here, Jack," he said and gave a cigar to Posey. "A good drink needs a good cigar."

Smalls reached for a match in the tinder-box, struck it, and lit Posey's cigar.

"So what brings you to Miles City?" Carver asked.

Carver and Smalls served with Posey and Spooner during the war and afterward, when Spooner recruited them; they rode with them until 'seventy-three when they had the good sense to call it quits.

"I'm looking for Tom, boys," Posey said.

Carver sighed loudly. "I had that feeling," he said.

"We been here since 'seventy-eight, Jack," Smalls said. "Tom only rode through once in all that time about a year ago. He loaded up on supplies and rode out the same day."

"I figured," Posey said. "I'm on my way to see Jane. I heard she has a ranch nearby."

"About twenty miles west," Smalls said. "She don't come to town but once every other month and not at all during winter."

"Is she all there in the head these days?" Posey asked.

"When has she ever been?" Smalls said.

"Jack, you ain't tracking old Tom alone, are you?" Carver asked.

"Want me to deputize you?" Posey asked.

"Shit, Jack," Smalls said. "I ain't worn my gun in so long I don't even know where it is."

117

"Same with me," Carver said. "We just ain't gunmen no more, Jack."

"I saw that right off by the soft bellies you two have grown," Posey said. "Now where can I get a hot bath, a good steak, and a soft bed?"

"There's six hotels and the like amount in boarding houses in town," Carver said. "We recommend the Black Rose."

"You wouldn't have some interest in that hotel?" Posey asked.

"We own it," Smalls said.

"And we don't charge old friends," Carver said.

"Give me some time to get cleaned up and I'll buy you gents a steak," Posey said.

"The hotel serves a good one," Carver said. "And it's on the house, Jack."

Posey let the bathhouse girl shave his face while he soaked in a tub of hot, soapy water.

He sipped coffee from a tin mug while she lathered and shaved him.

When his face was clean, the bathhouse girl said, "For an extra five dollars I'll hop in there and wiggle your bean for you good, Marshal."

"Five dollars?" Posey said. "What do they charge in the saloons?"

"Two, some girls as much as three."

"Then why do you charge five?"

" 'Cause those girls won't wash your back like I do."

"It's a tempting offer, but I have to respect the badge," Posey said.

"Well, if you change your mind, just ring that little bell there on the table beside the tub."

Posey met Carver and Smalls at six o'clock in the hotel dining room. Carver didn't lie when he said they served a good steak. It was one of the best Posey ever tasted.

"Montana is becoming cattle country, Jack," Carver said. "It's wide open and ripe for anyone with the capital and stock to start a ranch."

"You planning on doing that?" Posey asked.

"Us?" Smalls said. "We got too much going on around here to worry about ranching."

"Since you don't carry sidearms anymore, how do you two keep the peace?" Posey asked.

"We employ six deputies each," Smalls said. "They're younger and full of juice. We handle the paperwork and serving of warrants and such."

"Jack, when was the last time you had ice

cream?" Carver asked.

Posey thought for a moment. "I don't think I ever had no ice cream," he said.

"We got an ice cream maker came all the way from London in England," Carver said. "We have vanilla and chocolate and both are excellent."

"I'll order some for all of us after we finish our steak," Smalls said. "We'll take it on the porch."

Posey had to admit that ice cream was pretty damned good. He had a bowl with a scoop of chocolate and vanilla ice cream, covered with nuts and topped with a helping of whipped cream.

A mug of coffee to wash the sweetness down added to the pleasure.

"I have to admit ice cream is quite tasty," Posey said when his bowl was empty.

"Why don't you stay on here, Jack?" Smalls said.

"Most of our deputies are amateurs at best," Carver said. "A man like you can get rich in this country, Jack."

"It's cold as hell in these parts come November," Posey said.

"Nothing a good coat, a woman, and a warm fire can't fix," Carver said.

"I'll consider it right after I find Spooner,"

Posey said.

"Forget Tom Spooner," Smalls said. "Chasing him will only get you killed."

"Here comes one of your deputies," Posey said.

"He's one of mine," Smalls said.

The deputy came out of the dark street to the well-lit porch.

"Thought you should know, Sheriff, a fellow named Wil Stockburn is at the Last Chance," the deputy said. "He's wanted in Kansas for murder. He's playing cards and losing. Might be trouble."

"Is he wanted in Montana?" Smalls asked.

"No, sir, but he's wanted by the federal marshals," the deputy said.

"Are you sure?" Smalls asked.

The deputy rested his shotgun against the porch railing and dug a poster out of his shirt pocket and handed it to Smalls. "That ain't a drawing. It's a tinplate photograph. Came in last week in the mail."

Smalls held the poster up to the light of the wall-mounted lanterns, and then handed it to Posey.

"It's federal, Jack," Smalls said. "Makes it yours."

"I don't have time for this," Posey said.

"What should we do, Sheriff?" the deputy asked.

Smalls looked at Posey. "Jack?"

"Want I should round up the other deputies?" the deputy asked. "Two are already in the Last Chance."

Posey was suddenly on his feet and off the porch.

"I just had a bath," he said.

Posey quickly crossed the street and walked toward the Last Chance Saloon.

"Sheriff, we should back his play," the deputy said. "Shouldn't we?"

"Let's just watch," Smalls said. "Jack Posey don't need help from the likes of us."

Carver, Smalls, and the deputy left the porch and followed Posey to the Last Chance Saloon.

Holding the poster in his left hand, Posey pushed through the swinging doors and entered the crowded saloon.

Soldiers and cowboys made up most of the crowd. The piano player banged out an off-key tune. Two of Smalls's deputies stood at the bar.

Stockburn was playing poker with two soldiers and two cowboys at a table. From the looks of it, a soldier was the big winner and Stockburn a sore loser.

Posey pushed his way through the crowded saloon to the table where Stockburn sat and tossed the poster onto the table.

Stockburn looked at the poster and then grinned with yellow teeth at Posey.

"What in the hell do you want?" Stockburn said.

In one smooth, very quick motion, Posey drew his black Colt, flipped it around so he held it like a club, and smacked Stockburn across the face with it. The noise on contact was a loud thud and Stockburn fell over backwards, chair and all, to the floor.

The saloon was stunned into silence.

Posey looked at the two deputies at the bar. "Carry him over to the jail."

The deputies stared at Posey.

"You got mud in your ears?" Posey said. "Move."

The two deputies left the bar and walked to Stockburn.

Posey turned and walked to the swinging doors. He paused at the piano and looked at the man behind the keys.

"Learn how to play the goddamn piano," Posey said.

Posey sat behind Carver's desk in the jailhouse and wrote a telegram to the marshal in Dodge City, Kansas.

Smalls, Carver, and several deputies

gathered around the desk.

Posey handed the paper to a deputy. "Get this telegram sent right away to the marshal in Dodge," he said.

"Yes, sir," the deputy said and dashed out of the office.

"Mighty fine work, Jack," Carver said. "I wish you'd reconsider our offer."

"After I see Jane, I'll give it some thought," Posey said.

CHAPTER FOURTEEN

Posey was ready to ride at first light and walked his horse to the jailhouse where Smalls and Carver were seated outside in chairs. Each man had a mug of coffee.

"Have a cup with us before you go, Jack," Smalls said.

Posey tied his horse to the post and took the cup offered him by Carver. Smalls had a pot and filled the cup. Posey sat and rolled a cigarette.

"How do I find Jane?" Posey asked as he struck a match.

"Take the road out of town west," Carver said. "Stay west about twenty miles and you'll ride right into it. She has a small spread, horses mostly. Tell her to come to town more often."

"I will," Jack said and stood up. He set the cup on the seat and walked to his horse.

"Hey, Jack," Smalls said. "Watch yourself.

Old Tom ain't going to go lightly."

Posey rode ten miles and dismounted to give his back a rest from the saddle. He let the horse graze on thick Montana grass while he smoked a cigarette in the shade of a tree.

He skipped breakfast because he was still full from last night's large supper, but he felt a twinge of hunger now and dug out a large hunk of cornbread from his supplies and ate it with sips of water.

"All right, let's move," he told the horse.

Posey rode the remaining ten miles at a very slow pace. The morning sun was warm, and there didn't seem to be a need to hurry.

From a half mile away, he spotted Jane's cabin and corrals. He didn't see smoke rising from the chimney, but it was a warm morning so she probably didn't start a fire.

He rode to the cabin and dismounted at the corral. A dozen horses were penned inside, and a few foals were in a small, separate corral. Behind the cabin stood a red barn. Posey tied his horse at the corral and walked to the cabin.

Chickens pecked the dirt at his feet.

He stood at the base of the stairs of the porch.

"Jane Canary, you in there?" he shouted.

When there was no response, Posey went up to the porch.

"Martha Jane, it's Jack Posey," he shouted.

After a few seconds, he pushed in the unlocked door and poked his head inside the dark cabin.

Posey closed the door and took a chair on the porch. Next to the chair was a jug of corn liquor. He pulled the cork and took a sniff.

"God," Posey said and replaced the cork.

He rolled a cigarette and then removed the badge from his shirt and tucked it into a pocket.

After about an hour or so, Posey removed his hat and sat back in the chair with the warm sun on his face and began to doze off.

Footsteps and a rifle being cocked opened Posey's eyes.

Wearing dungaree pants, a long cloth coat, and carrying two hares and a Winchester rifle, Jane Canary looked at Posey. Her looks were gone now, but she still carried herself with the same self-assured confidence he remembered.

"Howdy, Jane," Posey said, standing up.

Jane squinted at him, then recognition set in and she rushed up the steps and hugged Posey.

"Jack Posey, I ain't seen you since Deadwood," Jane said.

"It's been a while, Jane."

Jane hung the hares over the porch railing and set the Winchester against the wall. "Sit down. Pull that cork. We need to drink a toast."

Posey pulled the cork and handed the jug to Jane. She took a long swallow and gave the jug to Posey.

He took a small sip. "That's god-awful stuff," he said.

"Ain't no better corn mash," Jane said. "So what are you doing this far north, Jack? I heard you got sent up to Yuma a few years back."

"I did, but the governor gave me a full pardon," Posey said.

"Pardon? How come?"

"They arrested me on the word of a liar when I was working at a ranch," Posey said. "Some cow bum said he recognized my black Colt, when I hadn't worn it in years. He said he saw me use it rustling some cows. Once they proved that a lie, I got pardoned."

"Damn," Jane said.

"So what are you doing out here, Jane?" Posey asked.

"Waiting on Texan Clinton Burke to come

up from Texas and marry me," Jane said. "We plan to move the ranch to Boulder, but he's a mite slow."

"Well, that's fine, Jane," Posey said.

"Sold eighty horses to the army at twenty-five dollars a head last year," Jane said. "This year be a hundred."

Jane took another swallow from the jug and then set it on the porch.

"So what brings you to these parts, Jack?" she asked.

"I'm looking for my old partner, Tom Spooner."

Jane stared at Posey for several seconds. "He ain't the man you knew back then, Jack," Jane said. "He's grown mean. Meaner than a mad rattler. You best stay clear of him."

"When did you last see him, Jane?" Posey asked.

"I ain't much to look at in the face no more," Jane said. "Not like in 'seventy-seven when you saw me in Deadwood, but my clam works just fine and if you give me a right worthy poke, I might be inclined to talk some."

"I thought you said you was waiting on that Texan?" Posey said.

"He left for Texas to gather a herd and been gone a year, the fool," Jane said. "So how about it, Jack? Seeing you here on my porch has got my clam to itching."

"Tell you the truth, Jane, you could use a bath," Posey said.

"What month is this?"

"May, almost June."

Jane shrugged.

"I'll go make a fire to boil some water," Jane said. "Put that big Bowie knife you got there to good use and skin them hares. Be careful, I save the pelts."

The white bathtub in the barn was elevated by a wheel on each corner and large enough for two people.

Posey sat in the hot, soapy water and looked at Jane as she got into the tub. Her body was all hard angles and muscle with little fat and curves like most city women have.

"Gimme the soap, Jack," Jane said. "I might as well get clean."

"Wash your hair, too," Posey said. "I could grease a wagon wheel axle with the grease in your hair."

Jane dunked under the water and when she came up, she said, "You're mighty particular for a man about to get a free poke, Jack, but at least you got the good sense not to call me Calamity."

"Good sense, hell," Posey said. "I just don't want to get shot is all."

Posey was sound asleep when he felt Jane rubbing herself against his leg and he opened his eyes.

"What are you doing, Jane?" he asked.

"What do you think I'm doing?" she said.

"Dammit, Jane, I was sleeping. Besides, you said you'd tell me what you know about Spooner if we had a poke, and then you fell asleep."

"Well I ain't asleep now and I want another poke," Jane said. "Otherwise I tell you nothing."

"Then will you answer my questions?"

"First thing in the morning," Jane said as she climbed on top of Posey.

Shirtless, wearing just his pants, Posey sat on the porch with a cup of coffee and a cigarette and let the morning sun warm his face.

After a time, wearing long underwear, Jane came out of the house and joined him. She also had a cup of coffee, but smoked a long-stemmed pipe.

"That was a fine breakfast, Jane," Posey said.

"Ain't no point keeping chickens if you

can't steal their eggs," Jane said. "Thanks for the bacon. Got anymore in your supply bag?"

"Some," Posey said. "You haven't lost your touch, Jane. When we met in Dora Du-Fran's brothel in Deadwood, I had no idea who you were back then. I do remember how sore I was after a visit, and I'm sore as hell right now."

"A girl had to make ends meet, especially after Wild Bill's passing," Jane said.

"I'm sorry I never got to meet the man," Jack said.

"You would have liked him, Jack," Jane said. "You're a lot alike in ways. He was tall like you and took nobody's shit, just like you, but never picked a fight that I know of. Ended a lot of them though, as I expect you have."

"Is it true you took a meat cleaver to Jack McCall's head after he shot Wild Bill?" Posey asked. "I read a story about that in a newspaper."

Jane grinned. "Well, shoot, Jack, I wished it were true, that little shit," she said. "But, no. They caught him and hung him with his boots off like he deserved."

"Well, Jane, let's talk," Posey said.

"I suppose," Jane said. "Old Tom rode through here about a year ago with his bunch of assholes. I told him they couldn't stay, but he said otherwise. They was running from the law and needed a place to rest up. They robbed a bank over in Rapid City and killed a few lawmen. I had no choice but to let them stay until their horses got their wind back. One of his men got the notion to crawl into bed with me during the night. I screamed and Tom woke up from where he bedded down near the fire and shot the man dead right there as if he were swatting a fly."

"Do you know which man it was Tom killed?" Posey asked.

"Not by name," Jane said. "A skinny fellow with a twitch. Had this hair so fine, it was almost white."

"That would be Phil 'Whitey' Johnson," Posey said. "He was harmless. He was a mite touched in the head, was all."

"What do you want with him for anyway?" Jane asked. "You looking to partner up with him again?"

"Not hardly," Posey said. "He owes me money from the old days. He was supposed to deliver it to me when I was punching cows and never did. I just want what's owed me is all."

"Money ain't worth dying for, Jack," Jane said. "Is it considerable?"

"Around twenty-two thousand I figure."

"Jack, Spooner ain't going to part with no twenty-two thousand, even if you did ride together," Jane said.

"I didn't say it would be easy," Posey said. "So tell me what you know about Tom Spooner."

"I know he'd shoot you on sight if you showed up asking for money," Jane said. "Even if it's owed you."

"Let me worry about that," Posey said.

Jane sucked on her pipe. "I hear he befriended Maybelle over to Fort Smith," she said. "We best go see her."

"I don't know any Maybelle," Posey said.

"Maybe you heard of her by her other name," Jane said. "Belle Starr."

"Newspapers call her the Queen of American Outlaws," Posey said.

"That would be her."

"Where can I find her?"

"You can't," Jane said. "But I can take you to her."

"I ride alone, Jane," Posey said. "I won't be responsible for someone else's life while I'm tracking Spooner."

"Then you won't get to see Belle, and you'll never find old Tom," Jane said.

"What about your Texan and this place?" Posey asked.

"We won't be gone that long, and I got a man coming to take the horses to the army," Jane said. "Should be here tomorrow."

"Well, where do we find Belle Starr?" Posey asked.

"Indian Nation in Arkansas," Jane said.

"Means we got to take the railroad," Posey said.

"I like the railroad, Jack. It's quicker than a month in the saddle," Jane said.

"Well, you got anything better to wear than those dirty pants and coat I saw you in yesterday?" Posey asked.

"I got a whole chest full of clothes," Jane said. "I just got no need of wearing them out here."

"You sure this Belle Starr knows Tom?" Posey asked.

"I'm sure."

"I guess we go see her then."

"Go split some wood. I got to boil some water."

"You just had a bath yesterday."

"To wash my clothes," Jane said. "I said I had 'em. I didn't say they was clean."

Posey stirred the clothes with an ax handle in the bathtub full of boiling hot water.

Jane came into the barn carrying a basket. "Let me have them undies, Jack," she said.

135

"For God's sake, Jane," Posey said.

"Never mind God and fetch my undies," Jane said.

Using the ax handle, Posey removed Jane's underwear from the tub and placed them into the basket.

"Might as well wash your own, Jack," Jane said. "No sense wasting good washing water."

Jack looked at the tub, then slowly removed his shirt, tossed it in, and stirred it with the ax handle.

By candlelight, Posey spread out a territorial map he got from Dale on the table.

Looking over his shoulder, Jane said, "We get the railroad in Miles City south all the way to Denver, and then go east to Missouri, and then south to Fort Smith. Shouldn't take us more than two and a half days at most."

"Your man will be here tomorrow?" Posey asked.

"Before ten," Jane said. "Now come to bed and give me a good poke, Jack."

Posey took a last look at the map, sighed, and blew out the candle.

Posey and Jane sat on the porch with cups of coffee and watched the rider approach the cabin from the east. He was a good half mile off and traveling at a leisurely pace.

"Is that your man?" Posey asked.

"That be Jose Manuel Ortega de Lobos Santiago," Jane said.

"Why is it every Mexican I ever met has six names?" Posey asked.

"I just call him Manny," Jane said.

"He sure don't hurry none, does he?"

"Got nothing to hurry for."

Ambling along at his slow pace, Manny finally arrived and dismounted at the corral. "I see you have company," he said in a thick Spanish accent.

"This is Jack Posey," Jane said. "Come have a cup of coffee. We need to talk."

Manny came up to the porch where Jane filled a cup with coffee.

"Sit," she said.

Manny took a chair and sipped from the cup.

"Me and Jack is taking a business trip down to Arkansas," Jane said. "I reckon I'll be gone close to two weeks. I want you and Jack here to gather up all the horses and bring them in. I figure we got close to sixty. After me and Jack leave tomorrow, you take them horses to the army and don't take less than twenty-five a head. You do and I'll skin you, you hear me?"

"What about the foals?" Manny asked.

"Take them to your place and watch them for me until I get back," Jane said. "Give your wife and eight kids something to do besides nag at you all day."

Manny looked at Posey. "Can you cowboy?"

"I can cowboy," Jack said.

"Then get off my porch and go do it," Jane said.

CHAPTER FIFTEEN

Posey proved to be a fair hand at cowboying, and by late afternoon, he and Manny had some sixty horses herded into the large corral.

"Jane is not here," Manny said when they tied their horses at the corral.

"Probably went hunting," Posey said.

"You cowboy pretty good for a man with a gun like that on his hip," Manny said.

"One's got nothing to do with the other," Posey said. "I got a pint bottle of good sipping whiskey in my gear. Let's go up to the porch, have a snort, and wait for Jane."

"My wife does not allow liquor in the house," Manny said as he and Posey went to the porch and took chairs. "I usually have to wait until I see Jane and drink that lantern oil she keeps in a jug."

Posey opened the pint bottle and handed it to Manny. "What they call Tennessee sipping whiskey," he said.

Manny took a small sip from the bottle. "Much better than Jane's sour mash," he said and passed the bottle to Posey.

Posey took a sip and nodded. "What they use to thin paint is better than her mash."

Posey handed the bottle to Manny and dug out his tobacco pouch. "You really have eight kids?"

"Nine, come this fall."

"How do you feed so many working horses?"

"I take horses to the army for six or seven local ranchers," Manny said. "Maybe five, six hundred head in a year. I get two dollars for each horse I take in. My wife, she has gardens and she grows all kinds of fruits and vegetables. Potatoes and corn and sometimes pumpkins."

"Pumpkins?"

"My wife, she fries them and also makes pies with them."

Posey struck a match and lit the cigarette.

"My wife doesn't allow tobacco in the house, too," Manny said.

Posey grinned and tossed Manny the pouch and papers. "She's a good Christian woman, huh?"

"No, a Mormon."

"Well, hell, she isn't going to stop until you got at least twenty running around,"

Posey said.

Jane came around the side of the cabin holding a large turkey.

"Ain't it just like men to waste time drinking whiskey when there's work to be done," she said.

"All the horses are in the corral," Manny said.

Jane slung the turkey over the porch railing and took a chair. "What have you got there, Jack?"

Posey handed Jane the bottle.

She read the label and then took three long swallows. "Never been to Tennessee," she said and handed the bottle to Posey.

Posey looked at the bottle. Jane had siphoned off a third and didn't as much as flinch.

"How many foals you bring in?" Jane asked.

"Seven," Manny said.

"Take all the foals to your place until I return," Jane said. "And have your two oldest come by every other day and gather up the chicken eggs. No sense letting them go to waste."

"I will do that," Manny said.

"Don't forget to cut your two dollars out when you sell 'em," Jane said.

"I won't forget," Manny said.

"Now take that turkey home to that crazy wife of yours before it gets dark," Jane said. "Or she might put some witch's spell on me."

"She's Mormon, not a gypsy, Jane," Manny said.

"I can't tell the difference," Jane said. "Now go."

Manny stood, took the turkey, and looked at Posey. "Maybe we can cowboy again sometime," he said.

"Maybe," Posey said.

After Manny rode away, Jane said, "Chop some wood, Jack. I'm going to have another bath so I'm clean for tomorrow."

"Hold still or I'll cut you for sure," Jane said.

"I don't see why a man can't shave his own damn face," Posey said.

" 'Cause I got no shaving mirror," Jane said as she ran the razor up Posey's neck.

They were in the bathtub and, to Posey's surprise, Jane had some French bubble bath she added to the hot water.

"There," Jane said. "Clean shaven. Rinse off."

Posey dunked under the water for a moment to rinse the shaving soap off his face.

When he came up, Jane said, "Grab that

little bottle there on the floor."

Posey reached for the tiny bottle beside the tub.

"That's hair soap they call shampoo," Jane said. "Came all the way from Paris in France. Pour a little on my hair and work it into a lather."

Posey removed the top from the bottle and poured a small amount on Jane's hair, replaced the top, and set the bottle on the floor.

Jane closed her eyes as Posey rubbed her hair.

"Jack, something I want to say," Jane said.

"What's that, Jane?"

"Why not stay here with me?" Jane said. "You're only going to get yourself killed chasing after Spooner."

"Jane, I'm not Wild Bill," Posey said as he worked the shampoo into a lather.

"I know that," Jane said. "Old Bill was going blind, Jack. Did you know that?"

"I did not."

"If that coward McCall didn't shoot him in the back of the head, Bill would have gone blind for sure," Jane said. "His eyes would hurt so bad sometimes, he'd smoke an opium pipe until he passed out to get rid of the pain."

"I'm sorry to hear that, Jane. Bill deserved

a better fate."

"So how about it, Jack? Why not stay here with me. It ain't so bad here, and when I set my mind to being true, I don't stray," Jane said.

"It's not that, Jane," Posey said. "My mind is set on Spooner. Rinse."

Jane dunked under to rinse her hair, came up, and said, "You'll just get yourself killed, Jack."

"It's the principle, Jane," Posey said. "A man don't sell out his principles."

"Oh, damn you, Jack Posey," Jane said. "Come here and give me a poke and to hell with your principles."

Chapter Sixteen

Posey waited on the porch for Jane after he saddled their horses. The morning sun was warm on his face as he drank some coffee and smoked a cigarette.

When she finally came out to the porch, he was shocked.

Jane wore a dark purple dress with black, high-button shoes and a purple hat with a feather in it. She didn't have her two-gun holster and carried a large satchel.

"Jane, you look fine," Posey said.

"Let's go if we're going, you stupid fool," Jane said.

They reached the outskirts of Miles City where Jane switched to riding sidesaddle.

When Posey looked at her, she said, "Ain't proper for a woman to be seen in public riding like a man."

As they rode down Main Street, everyone in town stopped to stare at them, not believing their eyes.

At the law office, Posey said, "Hold up a minute, Jane," and dismounted.

Carver and Smalls came out of the office and gawked at Jane.

"Good God, is that Calamity Jane?" Smalls said.

"Call me that again, and you'll find out firsthand why stupid people should never call me that," Jane said.

"No offense, Jane," Smalls said.

"Where you headed all dressed up like a schoolteacher?" Carver said.

"The railroad," Jane said and rode away.

Posey touched the brim of his black Stetson hat, and then followed Jane.

Seated in a riding car, Jane looked out the window at the darkness of night and said, "Let's go to our car and get some sleep, Jack. We got another ten hours to Denver."

"Why are you doing this, Jane?" Posey asked. "You could just tell me where to find Belle Starr and . . ."

"I told you, Jack. You'd never find her and if you did, you'd be dead inside ten seconds," Jane said. "I've grown fond of you. I'd hate to see you cut down in your prime like Wild Bill."

Posey dug out his tobacco pouch, paper,

and the pint bottle of bourbon. "Got enough left for a nightcap," he said.

"Roll one for me," Jane said.

Posey rolled two cigarettes and lit them both on a wood match and gave one to Jane.

"They'd cut down a man just for showing up?" Posey said as he took a sip from the bottle.

"In the first place . . . give me a shot of that," Jane said.

Posey handed the bottle to Jane and she took a sip.

"In the first place, Belle's hideout is secret from the law and is known only to a select few," Jane said. "Her lookouts even see a stranger headed their way, and they gun them down and investigate later."

"And they won't if I'm riding with you?"

"It's the only way you get to see Belle Starr, Jack."

"What's in this for you, Jane?"

"Tell you the truth, Jack, I'm wasting away waiting on that damned Texan," Jane said. "I needed to get out and stretch my legs."

"By sitting on a train for three days?"

Jane grinned, took a sip from the bottle, and passed it to Jack. "You'll get to stretch your legs in Fort Smith. Don't worry about that."

Posey took the last sip in the bottle and

said, "Damned train is about to rock me to sleep. Let's go to bed, Jane."

Jane stood up. "I think we can put the rocking of this train to good use," she said.

Fort Smith, Arkansas, was a large, bustling town with a population of more than three thousand people. Many buildings were constructed of red brick, including a large county courthouse presided over by Judge Isaac Parker.

"They call him the Hanging Judge," Jane said as they walked past the courthouse square.

A large clock in the courthouse tower read four-fifteen in the afternoon.

"We need to livery our horses and find a place to sleep," Posey said. "I'd like to leave at first light."

"We'll need supplies for two days," Jane said. "Livery is just down the street, and then we head over to Madam Poule's boarding house."

Madam Poule's boarding house was a combination boarding house for weary travelers and brothel for those less weary and in need of female companionship. The house had three floors, with floors one and two reserved for guests. The third floor, accessible from a separate, outside staircase, was the brothel.

Madam Poule was a plump woman in her fifties, with high cheekbones buffed to a shine with powder and bright red lips. Her ample breasts nearly popped out of her stylish and very tight blouse.

"Why Jane Canary, is that you?" Madam Poule said when Jane and Posey stepped onto her porch.

Seated in a wood rocking chair, Madam Poule stood up and gave Jane a hug.

"And who is this?" Madam Poule asked as she looked at Posey.

"Jack Posey, an old friend from Deadwood," Jane said.

"He doesn't look so old to me," Madam Poule said.

"Got a room for us?" Jane asked. "Just tonight."

"Got one on the second floor with a great big queen-size bed," Madam Poule said. "Room eleven. Supper is served at six. Two of my whores used to be chefs in some fancy restaurant in Chicago. They do all the cooking."

"See you at six," Jane said. "Jack, be a dear and grab my bag."

Holding his saddlebags and two rifles, Posey balanced them all and took hold of

Jane's satchel.

"Don't be late for supper," Madam Poule said.

Seated in the swing set on the front porch, Jane and Posey smoked cigarettes and drank after-dinner coffee. Wall-mounted lanterns glowed softly, providing gentle light.

"Those girls can cook," Jane said. "That was one fine beef stew."

"How long will it take us to reach Belle Starr?" Posey asked.

"Two days," Jane said. "We'll need supplies for two days, but buy enough for a week. And six bottles of good whiskey. No, better make it seven."

"We going to drink our way there?"

"No, silly," Jane said. "You don't show up at Belle's without an offering."

The two whores who prepared supper came out to the porch. "If you want a poke, we won't charge you double for the both of us," one of them said to Posey.

"If he wants a poke, it sure as hell won't be with you two skinny birds," Jane said. "Now get while you still got legs to walk with."

"Well, how about more coffee and dessert?" one of the whores asked.

"Do you have any ice cream?" Posey asked.

"No, but we baked an apple pie."

"That will do," Posey said.

Jane looked at Posey. "Ice cream, Jack?"

"I had some the other day in Miles City," Posey said.

"Speaking of pokes, I'm getting the itch again," Jane said.

"Can't it wait until after we had our pie?"

Jane stood and grabbed Posey's hand.

"Think of it as an exchange, Jack," she said. "One pie for another."

Shortly after sunrise, Posey retrieved the horses and walked them to the general store. It didn't open until eight, so he took a seat in a chair out front and smoked a cigarette while he waited.

The storekeeper and his wife arrived promptly at eight and opened for business. Posey bought enough supplies for a week and seven bottles of whiskey. With the horses loaded with supplies, he walked them to Madam Poule's boarding house.

Jane stood on the porch with a cup of coffee. She wore black trail pants with a dark blue shirt and black riding boots. Her two-gun holster was strapped around her thin waist.

"Madam Poule had her whores save us breakfast if you have an appetite," Jane said.

"How many miles we riding today?" Posey asked.

"Twenty, twenty-five, and all of them hard."

"Then I have an appetite," Posey said.

By noon, they were in the high country close to the Ozark Mountains.

"These foothills go on until dark," Jane said. "Tomorrow we start to climb. We'll be in the Indian Nation. Then we can start to worry."

"They aren't at war with anybody I know of," Posey said.

"Different kind of war, Jack," Jane said. "Let's find a stream and noon for a bit. My back hurts from this saddle."

Lunch was a simple meal of beans, bacon, and cornbread from the Forth Smith general store with coffee. Jane opened a bottle of whiskey and added some to her coffee cup.

"I'd suggest we hunt a turkey or hare for supper, but a shot carries for miles out here and we don't want any company in our sleep," Jane said.

"That store in Fort Smith had two beef-steaks wrapped in salt," Posey said. "We'll have them tonight. He also had this loaf of bread he said they make in the country of Italy. He called it Italian bread."

"I don't think I ever had no Italian bread," Jane said.

"He said it's good for soaking up gravy," Posey said.

Jane looked at the sky. "Finish up, Jack. We got six hours riding ahead of us."

Close to dark, they made camp near a small stream that ran down from the Ozarks.

"I don't know what hurts more, my back or my feet," Jane said.

"Go soak your feet in the stream while I build a fire and see to supper," Posey said.

Posey built a fire, put up the beans and coffee, and then tended to the horses. By the time he put the steaks in the fry pan, the coffee was ready, and he took a cup to the stream where Jane was soaking her feet.

"I ain't cut out for this kind of life no more, Jack," Jane said. "I ain't young like I was them years in Deadwood. I reckon when I get home, I'll wire that damn Texan and see what's holding him up."

"Sounds like a wise decision," Posey said.

"Maybe you should make a wise decision yourself," Jane said.

"If you mean forget about Tom Spooner, I can't do that," Posey said.

"No, I reckon you can't," Jane said. "Being a stubborn fool and all."

"I best see to those steaks," Posey said.

"This Italian bread is hard as rock," Jane said.

"Rip off a piece and wipe up the juice from the steak," Posey said. "It's pretty good that way."

Jane tore off a small piece of the bread and soaked up the juice from her steak and then placed it in her mouth. "Ain't so bad when it's wet," Jane said. "Where is this Italian country anyway?"

"Italy is a country in Europe," Posey said. "I studied about the Roman Empire in school. They used to rule the world at one time."

"Maybe so," Jane said. "But they make lousy bread."

"Where are we headed tomorrow?" Posey asked.

"High country," Jane said. "And I hope you ain't afraid of the dark."

CHAPTER SEVENTEEN

By early afternoon they had covered close to twenty miles in rough, high country. Jane seemed to know where every pass and turn was located, and they had little trouble making distance.

"Hold up, Jack," Jane said as they reached a pass through a rocky gorge surrounded by mountains.

Jane and Posey dismounted.

"It's a hard climb here on out," Jane said. "The horses need rest and grain, and I'm a mite hungry, too."

"We got five hours of daylight left," Posey said. "We'll rest an hour."

"I'll have some of that cornbread if there's any left," Jane said.

"Got a whole loaf," Posey said.

After crossing through the pass, Jane led the way to high country.

"We in the Ozarks now, Jack," she said.

"It's pretty country," Posey said. "Reminds me of Colorado or Utah some."

Jane reached into a saddlebag for a brightly colored necklace and placed it around her neck.

"What's that for?" Posey asked.

"Belle gave it to me," Jane said. "If they see this, they won't cut us down."

"What is it?"

"Sign of the Cherokee Nation, Jack."

The sun had shifted across the sky, and by four in the afternoon the ground was covered in shadow.

Posey kept his eyes scanning the high ground. At one point he spotted sunlight reflecting off something shiny in the mountains.

"Did you see that, Jane?" Posey asked.

"I saw it."

"Sun reflecting off the metal on a rifle," Posey said.

"I know," Jane said.

"It's at least a mile off," Posey said.

"We'll ride to dark," Jane said. "Tomorrow you get to meet Belle Starr."

A few minutes before dawn, Posey untangled himself from Jane's body and got out of the bedroll. Even though it was early July, the higher elevation of the Ozarks brought a chill to the morning.

He built a fire and put coffee on to boil. Breakfast would be beans, bacon, and cornbread. When the coffee was ready, Jane awoke and sat up.

"Is that coffee I smell?" she said.

"It is. Have a cup. Breakfast is nearly ready," Posey said.

"Roll me one of those cigarettes, Jack," Jane said.

Posey rolled a cigarette, lit it, and passed it to Jane, along with a cup of coffee.

"How long to reach Belle?" Posey asked.

"From here about four hours," Jane said. "And from here you ride blindfolded."

"Is that necessary?"

"Only if you want to reach Belle Starr alive," Jane said.

Jane led Posey's horse with a rope looped around his neck and tied to her saddle horn. Jane also tied Posey's hands behind his back to keep him from removing the bandanna she wrapped around his eyes. With his eyes blindfolded, Posey had no notion of direction, just that they were traveling up.

Sometime after noon — Posey could tell by the sun on his face — Jane stopped the horses and dismounted.

She untied Posey's hands and he removed the bandanna. The sun was blinding for a few moments until his eyes adjusted to the light.

"A quarter mile and we're there," Jane said as she removed the rope from Posey's horse.

Jane mounted her horse and said, "There's three riders behind us and the like number on our flanks. We go in easy and there will be no trouble."

"Lead the way," Posey said.

The trail evened out after a few hundred yards to a grass-filled clearing. Posey spotted rising smoke about a thousand yards in the distance.

"Our destination," Jane said.

As they neared the two cabins and corral in the distance, three riders appeared behind Posey and Jane.

When they were five hundred feet away, three riders on each flank appeared, and the nine riders escorted Posey and Jane to the large corral where a dozen or more horses were penned.

Belle Starr and two men were seated in chairs on the porch of the first cabin.

"Stay in the saddle until Belle says so," Jane said.

Belle stood up and said, "Jane Canary,

climb down off that horse and bring your companion."

Jane and Posey dismounted.

"Bring the whiskey, Jack," Jane said as she walked to the porch.

Posey removed the wood box wrapped in fishnet and tied to the back of Jane's saddle.

Jane stepped up onto the porch and looked at Belle.

"Howdy, Belle. You look fine," Jane said.

"It's been too long, Jane," Belle said.

"At least a year."

"Still raising horses for the army in Miles City?"

"For now. I'm waiting on the Texan to come north and marry me," Jane said.

Belle looked at Posey. "And who is this?"

"Jack Posey," Jane said. "An old friend from Deadwood."

"What have you got there, Jack Posey?"

"A gift, Belle," Jane said.

"Bring your gift on up here, Jack Posey," Belle said.

Posey went up to the porch and set the wood box on the floor in front of Belle.

"Open it, Jack," Jane said.

Posey removed the fishnet and then drew his Bowie knife and pried open the lid of the crate.

Jane removed one bottle of whiskey and

showed it to Belle.

"Well, dammit girl, pass that here," Sam Starr said.

"Be quiet, you old fool," Belle said and took the bottle. "From Tennessee. Thank you, Jane. We haven't had any good whiskey around here in quite a spell."

"That's a mighty fine piece you got there, mister," the very large man seated next to Sam Starr said, looking at Posey's Colt.

"It is," Posey said.

"I'll draw you for it," the man said.

"No thank you," Posey said.

"Then I'll just take it," the man said.

"I don't advise that," Posey said.

"You don't, huh?"

"Oh, be quiet," Belle said. She looked at Posey. "That big Cherokee is Sha-con-gah, otherwise known as Blue Duck."

Posey looked at Blue Duck. "I've heard of him," he said.

"Are you the Jack Posey some call Lightning Jack?" Belle asked.

"Some call me that," Posey said. "I never liked it, though."

Belle looked at Blue Duck. "Still want to draw him?"

"Talk don't mean shit," Blue Duck said.

"Give me that bottle, Belle," Sam said.

Blue Duck stood up and put his right

160

hand on his gun, but before he could pull it, Posey had his Colt out, cocked, and pressed against Blue Duck's stomach.

"I didn't come here to kill nobody," Posey said. "But I won't be wronged by no man, Cherokee or otherwise."

"Sit down, you stupid Cherokee, before you get your guts blown all over the porch," Belle said.

Glaring at Posey, Blue Duck took his chair.

Posey holstered his Colt.

"I read in the newspaper they locked you up in Yuma a few years back," Belle said.

"They did, but I got a pardon," Posey said. "Seems the man who testified against me lied in court."

"Belle, the bottle," Sam said.

Belle gave the bottle to Sam and said, "Take Blue Duck with you and go get drunk somewhere. Me and Jane have some talking to do."

Sam and Blue Duck left the porch and walked to the corral where the men waited.

"Sit," Belle said as she took her chair. "Let's talk some."

Posey and Jane took chairs next to Belle.

"The glow on your cheeks tells me you've had some good pokes recently," Belle said as she looked at Posey.

"The Texan's been gone a year, Belle," Jane said. "A girl gets lonely, you know."

At the corral, the men were whooping loudly as Sam passed the bottle around.

"Men are such useless creatures except for that bean between their legs," Belle said. "If it weren't for that, they'd have no purpose at all."

"Maybe so, Belle, but Jack here is the resourceful type," Jane said.

Belle looked at Posey. "Let's take a walk, Jack Posey," she said.

Belle led Posey and Jane off the porch to the side of the cabin and around back. Not far from the cabins was a one-square-acre garden of vegetables. Belle led them toward the garden.

"We got potatoes, carrots, squash, and even corn growing there," Belle said. She pointed to a coop structure on the left a hundred yards away. "Got three dozen chickens for eggs and even some cows for milk and beef down yonder."

Belle kept walking toward the vegetable garden and stopped at the edge.

"We can stay here for years if we have to," she said. "And we might have to. Judge Parker issued a warrant on me for crimes I didn't commit, and he'd surly love to hang me and Sam if he got the chance."

"I'm sorry to hear that, Belle," Jane said.

Belle nodded. She wore a dark blue skirt with a matching blouse and black boots. A brown belt circled her waist, but she wore no guns.

"So let's find out what you want, Jack Posey," Belle said. "Because you didn't come all this way and risk your life just to bring me some sipping whiskey."

Posey knelt down and touched the young cornstalks.

"If you add some horse or cow manure to the soil, it increases production," he said. "You'll get a lot more growth without using more land."

"You know about farming?" Belle asked.

Posey stood up. "Before the war took everything, my family had a three-hundred-acre spread. I worked it for years."

"I didn't know that," Jane said. "I figured you were always a gunman."

"The war was hard on all of us," Belle said. "My family lost the farm in Missouri soon after, and times were hard. That's why I married my first husband, a no-account named Jim Reed."

"I didn't know you was from Missouri, Belle," Jane said.

"I'm a Missouri man myself," Posey said. "Never had the need to cross the border into Arkansas back then."

"But you do now," Belle said.

"Jack is looking for Tom Spooner and his bunch," Jane said.

Belle looked at Posey. "Why?"

"We rode together more than ten years, counting the war," Posey said. "Before we split up we amassed a tidy sum of money. I never got my share even though we agreed to an even split. He arranged for that witness to testify against me for the reward money, then after had the witness killed. I just want what's mine, what's owed."

"Why did you split up after so many years?" Belle asked.

"Tom changed," Posey said. "Killing was necessary during the war, but after he got so that he enjoyed it. He shed blood just for the sake of doing it. I'm not that way. Never was."

"What do you figure Tom Spooner owes you, Jack Posey?" Belle asked.

"I put the sum at twenty-two thousand dollars," Posey said.

"Tom Spooner ain't going to part with no twenty-two thousand dollars, Jack Posey," Belle said. "Even if he had it, which I doubt he does."

"Well, I need to find out," Posey said. "One way or the other."

"And you think I can help you?" Belle said.

"I told him you could, Belle," Jane said.

"I see you have a pouch in your shirt pocket," Belle said. "Fix me a cigarette if you please."

Posey dug out pouch and papers and rolled three cigarettes. He gave one each to Belle and Jane and lit all three off a wood match.

"I met Spooner through Charles Younger in 'seventy-eight," Belle said. "Spooner was crazy then and worse now. You can see it in his eyes, the madness. However, he ain't stupid. You go to hunting him and he's likely to kill you, Jack Posey."

"I'll take my chances," Posey said.

"He's come here several times in the past few years when the law was dogging him, and I gave him sanctuary," Belle said. "Even my bunch was scared of him and his group, and that's saying a lot."

"Then why give him sanctuary?" Posey asked.

"Ten percent of your loot," Belle said. "That's my going rate for sanctuary. He didn't want to pay it, but he had no choice. I have thirty guns to his eight and he didn't fancy a shootout."

"When did you see him last?" Posey asked.

"March."

"Can you tell me how I can find him?"

"Let's go back to the cabin," Belle said. "The boys will want supper, and I have two birds hanging in the kitchen. We'll talk more about Tom Spooner later."

After supper, with the sun quickly setting, Belle, Sam, Jane, and Posey sat on the porch while most of the men hung out down by the corral.

"You can have the extra bed in my cabin for the night," Belle said. "It's lumpy, but better than sleeping on the ground."

"Let's crack open another bottle," Sam said.

"One bottle today is quite enough," Belle said. "We'll have coffee. Jane, will you see if it's ready?"

Jane went inside the cabin.

"Sam, go see what the men are up to," Belle said.

Sam stood and left the porch.

"So Jack Posey, let's talk some," Belle said.

Posey rolled a cigarette, lit it, and gave it to Belle.

"If I tell you how you might find Spooner, he might just show up here and try to kill me," Belle said.

"Only if I told him you told me how to

find him," Posey said. "And only if he kills me before I kill him."

"You'd be better off trying to waltz with the devil," Belle said.

"Maybe so, but let me ask you this: at what point would you quit looking for your twenty-two thousand dollars?" Posey asked.

Belle looked at Posey and nodded.

Jane returned with the coffee pot and three cups. She gave a cup to Belle and Posey and poured, then sat.

"On the other side of the Rio Grande, just past Laredo, is a border town called Nuevo," Belle said. "Spooner bragged about he practically owned the place. A bunch of dirt-poor farmers in a small village, but there is a Mexican girl there Spooner is sweet on. Says he aims to marry her one day. Find that girl, and you find Spooner."

"What's her name?" Posey asked.

"Spooner called her Pilar Lobos. To hear Spooner talk of her, she's quite the stargazer in the looks department," Belle said.

"I'm obliged to you, Belle," Posey said.

"If you manage to live, Jack Posey, you come back and see me," Belle said. "And bring me ten percent of your loot."

Blue Duck came to the porch.

"I'll be leaving now, Belle," he said.

"It's dark," Belle said.

"Good moon. Night riding don't bother me none," Blue Duck said.

"See you next time you ride through," Belle said.

Blue Duck glared at Posey for a moment, then turned and walked to the corral where his saddled horse waited.

"I almost married that filthy savage," Belle said. "Although Sam ain't much better when he's drunk."

"Most men aren't worth spit anyway," Jane said.

"Come inside, Jack Posey," Belle said. "I'll show you where you and Jane can sleep."

Posey woke up alone in the middle of the night and looked at the lone candle burning on the table on the other side of the cabin.

From the bedroom, he heard Sam Starr snoring.

And soft whispering coming through the screen door.

Posey quietly got out of bed and inched his way to the screen door. The moon was bright enough for him to see that Belle sat in a chair and Jane was on her lap with her face resting against Belle's chest.

"They killed him, Belle," Jane sobbed. "The coward McCall killed my Bill, and I was there to see him do it. Why, Belle?"

"There are no answers, Jane," Belle said. "Men are violent creatures by nature, even the good ones. We live with it because we have no choice but to live with it."

"Maybe I could have done something?" Jane said. "But Bill was stubborn to a fault when it came to his cards."

"There was nothing you could do, Jane. It was fate," Belle said. "What about your Texan?"

"A poor second choice, Belle."

"And Posey?"

"That's all I need is to fall for another fool looking for an early grave, damn him," Jane said. "I expect I'll just wait on the Texan to show up and marry me."

Posey turned away from the screen door and quietly returned to bed. After a while he fell asleep and when sunlight on his face opened his eyes, Jane was snuggled against his back.

Chapter Eighteen

After breakfast, Posey saddled his horse and then met Jane and Belle on the porch of her cabin.

"Roll me one of those cigarettes, Jack Posey, and join us for a farewell cup of coffee," Belle said.

Posey dug out his pouch and papers, rolled three cigarettes, and lit them with a wood match. After he gave one to Belle and Jane, he took a chair and Jane filled a cup with coffee from the pot.

"You'll be headed down to Mexico then," Belle said.

"I will be," Posey said.

"Go on and get yourself killed," Jane said. "You'll get no sympathy here."

"Remember what I said about Spooner, Jack Posey," Belle said. "You'll likely be waltzing with the devil himself."

"I'll remember," Posey said.

"Oh, damn you," Jane said, then stood up

and went into the cabin.

"Some women don't like long goodbyes," Belle said. "Best be on your way. My men will escort you safely to lower ground."

Posey nodded, set the cup down, and returned to his horse. He mounted the saddle and looked back at Belle.

"Tell Jane goodbye and thanks," he said.

Belle waved. "I will," she said. "And good luck."

Blindfolded and led by three of Belle's men down to lower ground, Posey felt bad about leaving Jane the way he did, but what was he to do?

He didn't love Jane and even if he did, he was not about to be a poor substitute for Wild Bill Hickok's affections.

After an hour or so in the saddle, Belle's men stopped and one of them said, "Take the mask off. You're free to go."

Posey removed the bandanna from his eyes and nodded to the men as one of them removed the rope from his horse's neck.

"Adiós," Posey said.

Posey rode down the mountain for several hours and was lost in thought. He needed to resupply in Fort Smith before . . .

The attack came from the rocks above his

head as he rode through a narrow pass. That the pass was narrow probably saved Posey's life as, when Blue Duck knocked him out of the saddle, Blue Duck hit the rocks hard and the knife in his hand fell from his grasp.

Both men were stunned for a few seconds from the hard fall. Posey recovered first and stood up. Blue Duck slowly stood up a few seconds later. He looked around for his knife, but it was out of arm's reach.

"I've done you no harm. What is it you want?" Posey asked.

"I told you, I want that Colt," Blue Duck said.

"You just take what you want?" Posey said.

"Doesn't everybody?"

"Well, I'll give you what you want," Posey said.

Blue Duck realized he had no chance in a draw with Posey and made a sudden charge at him; Posey drew the Colt, flipped it around, and smacked Blue Duck in the jaw with it.

The big Cherokee went down, but he wasn't out. Posey clubbed him two more times and Blue Duck fell unconscious.

Posey holstered the Colt and mounted his horse. He backtracked for a bit and found Blue Duck's horse tied to a tree off the path. He took the reins of Blue Duck's horse, led him down the mountain, and didn't release him until they reached flat ground hours later.

"Well, look who's returned," Madam Poule said when Posey rode to the porch of her boarding house.

Posey dismounted, stretched his back, looped the reins around the hitching post, and went up to the porch.

"Got a vacant room for the night?" Posey asked.

"I have," Madam Poule said. "Do you want a bath and a woman?"

"Just a bath and something decent to eat," Posey said.

"Bring in your gear, and I'll have the girls draw a bath," Madam Poule said. "Want your clothes washed?"

"I do."

"Second door on the right on the second floor," Madam Poule said.

One of Madam Poule's whores shaved Posey's face while he soaked in a tub of hot, soapy water.

"I ain't allowed to give you a free one although I'd like to," the whore said. "The shave is an extra four bits."

"I don't want a free one," Posey said. "All

I want is some decent food and about ten hours' sleep."

"Your face is clean. Dunk under," the whore said.

Madam Poule invited Posey to dine with her in her private quarters. Her two girls served steak with all the fixings.

"What become of Jane?" Madam Poule asked.

"She decided to stay and visit a while with Belle Starr," Posey said.

"Belle hasn't been seen in Fort Smith in a year since Judge Parker issued a hanging warrant on her," Madam Poule said.

"She told us," Posey said.

"Where are you headed next?" Madam Poule asked.

"South."

"Want to stay put a spell?"

"Here?"

"Things have been kind of rough lately," Madam Poule said. "A lot of cowboys off the trail and such. Been some trouble, and Judge Parker said he'd close me down if things don't quiet down. I'll give you a room, three squares a day, twenty-five dollars a week, and one free poke a night to keep the peace."

"It's a kind offer, but I have to move on

tomorrow. I have pressing business," Posey said.

Madam Poule sighed. "If you change your mind, you let me know in the morning," she said.

Posey didn't change his mind. At ten o'clock the next morning, he was on a train west to Santa Fe in New Mexico.

CHAPTER NINETEEN

Sarah and Erin were cracking beans on the front porch when Posey rode up to the house and dismounted.

"Ma, it's Uncle Jack," Erin said.

"I see him, honey," Sarah said. "Go inside and fetch your father."

Erin set aside her bowl and went into the house.

"Can I come up?" Posey asked.

"Come on," Sarah said.

Posey went up to the porch and removed his hat.

"I was mad enough to shoot you myself, Jack," Sarah said. "But when Dale told me what you did, that you saved his life, I promised myself I would do this instead the next time I saw you."

Sarah set her bowl aside, stood, and engulfed Posey in a big hug.

The screen door opened and Dale limped out with the aid of a cane.

"Trying to steal my wife, Jack?" Dale said.

Sarah released Posey. "Be quiet, you big dope," she said.

Dale and Posey shook hands.

"We have some talking to do," Dale said.

"Reckon so," Posey said.

Alone on the porch, Posey and Dale had fresh cups of coffee. Posey smoked a cigarette while Dale smoked his father's pipe.

"I remember Dad smoking that old pipe," Posey said.

"Calamity Jane and Belle Starr, Jack?" Dale said. "Jesus."

"Jane hates being called Calamity, and Belle Starr is a right fine woman," Posey said. "Sam Starr doesn't want to do much except get drunk. I met Blue Duck along the way."

"That outlaw? What happened?"

"He took a fancy to my Colt," Posey said. "I had to set him straight on the matter."

"I can imagine how you did that," Dale said.

"The trail to Spooner leads south to Old Mexico," Posey said. "I'll be leaving as soon as my horse is rested."

"I'm two or three weeks away from hard riding, Jack," Dale said.

"I'm not asking you to go with me," Posey said. "All I need is to resupply and some expense money."

"It can't wait?"

"I don't think so."

Dale sighed. "At least take a few deputies."

"They'll just slow me down and I told you, I won't be responsible for another man's life."

"God, you're stubborn," Dale said.

"So was Ma, if you recall," Posey said.

"Where's your badge?"

"My pocket," Posey said. "I couldn't very well ride in to see Belle Starr and her clan wearing it."

"I suppose not," Dale said. "When do you figure to head out?"

"I'd like to rest up my horse for another day," Posey said. "I've grown right fond of him."

"Tomorrow we'll go to the office and I'll swear out official warrants and see about expense money," Dale said. "If it takes long enough for you to track him down, I can probably join you on the road."

Sarah opened the screen door and stepped onto the porch.

"If you men want supper, now is the time," she said.

■ ■ ■ ■

From the front porch, the lights of a very awake Santa Fe glowed brightly. Even faint piano music could be heard. Dale, Sarah, and Posey sat in chairs to take in the cooler night air.

"This is a right nice town," Posey said. "I see why you settled here."

"You missed the Fourth of July celebration we had a few days ago," Dale said. "The whole town showed up. The mayor hired a professional pyrotechnician from back east to put on a fireworks show right on Main Street."

"Tomorrow is Sunday," Sarah said. "There will be our annual fried chicken picnic after services. I expect you to attend."

"Of course," Dale said.

"I meant your brother," Sarah said.

"He knows what you meant, honey," Dale said. "I was just fooling with you."

"Service is at ten," Sarah said. "I'm going to see to the children and turn in. Don't you men stay up late talking foolishness. I won't abide grown men falling asleep in church."

After Sarah went inside, Posey rolled a cigarette.

"I saw a telegram last week that said you arrested Wil Stockburn in Miles City," Dale said.

"I was on my way to see Jane," Posey said. "It just came up."

"Well, that was good work," Dale said. "Maybe you'd like to keep that badge permanently?"

Posey looked at Dale.

"I best join Sarah," Dale said.

"I'll be in shortly," Posey said.

Alone on the porch, Posey finished his cigarette and coffee before deciding to turn in for the night.

Posey sat in a front row pew with Dale, Erin, and John while Sarah conducted the hour-long service. The church was packed and Posey wasn't sure if that was due to Sarah's fire and brimstone sermon, or the free fried chicken that was to follow.

Shortly after the service, the congregation gathered behind the church in the large garden where several picnic tables had been set up. While the women gathered the food and set the tables, the men clustered in groups and the children played.

Girls jumped rope; boys played marbles and the game called tag. The men talked politics of the day.

"Uncle Jack, would you play catch with me?" John asked Posey.

"I don't know what that is," Posey admitted.

"When they played baseball last month, I got to keep a ball used during the games," John said and produced a worn baseball from his pocket. "We just sort of toss it back and forth."

Posey took the ball and inspected it. "The ball has changed some since I last saw it during the war," he said. "Let's move away from the tables."

Posey and John engaged in a game of catch on the side of the church until Sarah called them to the tables.

"We'll take a walk over to the office after we're done eating," Dale said.

Dale limped to his desk and took the chair, resting his cane against the wall.

"Something you should know," he said to Posey.

Dale slid open a desk drawer and removed some documents. "Official warrants from the Justice Department in Washington on Tom Spooner," he said. "And this."

Posey picked up the second warrant. "Pepper Broussard," he said. "When did that scum take up with Spooner?"

"They robbed a bank in Boise just last week," Dale said. "People in town claimed they recognized Broussard from his wanted posters."

"Boise?" Posey said. "That's far west."

Dale nodded. "They killed three more people, Jack," he said. "We sent six federal marshals to Boise just the other day."

"They won't find them."

"I expect not," Dale said. "Jack, Broussard is suspected of killing at least twenty men, maybe even more."

"I never thought Spooner was running with a Sunday school bunch, Dale," Posey said. "Pepper Broussard is just the sort I figured Spooner would recruit."

"I didn't dissuade you, did I?"

"No."

Dale sighed. "Take those warrants," he said.

Posey folded the warrants and stuck them in his shirt pocket.

Dale dug out a small strongbox from the bottom desk drawer. "You'll need expense money," he said and removed one thousand dollars. "And sign for it."

Posey signed the expense book and then pocketed the money.

"I hear fiddle music," Dale said. "Maybe you might like to dance with my wife."

■ ■ ■ ■

Sarah was a delightful dancer and danced with Posey to several different songs.

When they took a break for some punch at the table where Dale sat, Erin approached Posey.

"Would you like to dance with me, Uncle Jack?" she asked.

"I sure would," Posey said.

While the fiddler played a waltz, Posey danced with Erin to the delight of the crowd.

Posey sat on the front porch after the evening meal. He had a cup of coffee and was about to roll a cigarette when Erin opened the screen door and came out.

"I thought you went to bed," Posey said.

"Ma said I could say goodnight," Erin said.

"Well, goodnight, sweetheart," Posey said.

"I wanted to thank you for dancing with me," Erin said.

"It was my pleasure."

"You will come back?"

"Sure, I'll be back," Posey said.

"Promise me."

"I promise."

Erin went over and gave Posey a tight hug. "Good," she said.

"Now you best get to bed."

"Goodnight, Uncle Jack," Erin said and went inside.

Posey rolled a cigarette, lit it with a wood match, and was alone with his thoughts.

Chapter Twenty

Posey stood beside his horse and shook Dale's hand.

"Sorry I can't go with you, Jack," Dale said.

"It's better this way," Posey said.

Sarah stood with Erin and John on the porch. Erin was crying, and Sarah was nearly in tears herself.

"I don't see why you have to go at all," Sarah said.

Dale looked at her.

"We been over this, Sarah," he said.

"Well go on and get yourself killed then, you damn fool," Sarah said.

"Mama, you swore," Erin said.

"And I'll swear again if I feel like it," Sarah said.

Dale sighed. "Put your badge on, Jack," he said.

Posey dug out the badge and pinned it to his shirt.

"Watch yourself, Jack," Dale said.

Posey mounted his horse, looked at Sarah, and tipped his hat.

"I'll be back if for nothing else than your fried chicken and one more dance," he said.

After a day and a half on trains, the best the railroad could do was take Posey to Houston, Texas.

It was an enormous city of sixteen thousand people, due mostly to the fact that it was the hub of the railway system in the state. The railroad yard was the largest Posey had ever seen and dwarfed the yard he saw when he visited Saint Louis years ago.

He retrieved his horse from the boxcar and walked the tenth of a mile from the railroad yard to the edge of town. There were horse-drawn carriages to take passengers from the station into town. Posey was astounded at the height of the buildings, some reaching heights of ten or more stories.

People were everywhere, walking the streets and riding in carriages. A few cowboys were on horseback, but not many. Even though it was just noon, saloons were open on nearly every block.

People on wood sidewalks stared at Posey as he walked his massive black horse along the streets. On the corner of a street, a police officer wearing a blue uniform, armed with a short-nosed revolver and a nightstick, approached Posey. A whistle dangled from a cord around his neck.

"Firearms aren't permitted inside the city limits," the police officer said.

Posey moved his vest and displayed the US marshal's badge.

"Sorry, Marshal, I didn't see your badge."

"Where can I find the federal marshal's office?" Posey asked.

"Six blocks ahead and two blocks over," the police officer said. "The courthouse building, second floor."

"Obliged."

Posey was impressed by the size of the courthouse building. It was constructed of red brick with white stone steps and had a corral on the side for visitors to leave their horses. An attendant guarded the horses.

"Do you see that Winchester and Sharps rifle on my horse?" Posey asked the attendant.

"Yes, Marshal."

"If they're not there when I return, somebody will be kicked up and down Main Street," Posey said.

"No need to worry, Marshal."

187

The interior of the courthouse was all polished wood with fancy office doors with etched glass and names picked out in gold lettering. A staircase took Posey to the second floor where he found the federal marshal's office.

Gold lettering in the etched glass read: M. Clinton United States Marshal.

Posey opened the door and entered the office. A woman sat behind a large desk. On the desk was a typewriter and telegraph. She was typing and looked up at Posey.

"Can I help you?" she asked.

"Deputy Marshal Posey. Is Marshal Clinton available?" Posey said.

The woman looked at Posey's badge. "From?"

"Santa Fe."

She stood up and went down a hallway. Posey looked at the photographs on the wall, mostly of Houston in various stages of growth.

The woman returned and said, "This way, Deputy."

Posey followed her down a long hallway, passing several more desks and offices to a door marked US Marshal Clinton. She opened the door and stepped aside to allow Posey to enter.

The office was large, with a desk, file

cabinets, and even a rug. Behind the desk, Clinton stood. He was a short, balding man in his forties, and he wore a suit like a city banker.

"Are you Marshal Clinton?" Posey asked.

"I am," Clinton said. "How can I help you, Deputy?"

"Tom Spooner, know of him?" Posey asked.

"Of course I know of him," Clinton said. "He isn't in my territory or I'd have every man I got out looking for him."

"I have warrants from Washington for his arrest," Posey said.

"How many with you?"

"Just me."

"Just you? Are you crazy?"

"Probably."

"If you're looking for help, I can't give you any," Clinton said. "I have a territory twice the size of Rhode Island and just twenty-four men to police it. Texas is full of horse thieves, murderers, bank robbers, and bandits and I can't spare a man to . . ."

"I'm not asking for your help," Posey said.

"Then why are you here?"

"Tom Spooner picked up a new man, a Texan named Pepper Broussard," Posey said. "What can you tell me about him?"

"That one," Clinton said. He came around

from behind his desk and went to a large file cabinet against the wall. He opened a drawer and removed a file. "Originally from San Antonio. Born in 'fifty-one. Wanted in Texas for horse stealing, cattle rustling, murder, rape, barn-burning, card-cheating, and just about everything else you can name. Here's a sketch of him."

Posey looked at the sketch.

"He has gold-colored hair and a scar on his left cheek," Clinton said.

"I hear he's good with a gun," Posey said.

"Reports say no one is better," Clinton said. "At one time he worked as an enforcer for Judge Roy Bean in a makeshift court-room in a saloon near Eagle's Nest. Bean is a duly appointed justice of the peace, but calls himself 'judge.' Folks in those parts call him the hanging judge."

"Thanks for the information, Marshal," Posey said.

"You're not seriously going after Spooner's bunch alone?" Clinton said.

"Seems that way," Posey said. "Unless you want to give me a dozen or so of your men."

Clinton stared at Posey.

"No, I guess not," Posey said. "I'll see myself out."

At the front desk, the woman was typing again and Posey paused to look at her.

"What is that thing?" he asked.

"This? It's a typewriter," she said. "All the newspapers have them now to write their stories on. We use it so there are no mistakes caused by poor handwriting or grammar."

Posey looked at the telegraph on the desk.

"Can you work that thing?" he asked.

"Of course. They say in ten years the telephone will replace the telegraph in every newspaper and courthouse in the country."

"They say that, huh," Posey said.

The woman looked at Posey.

He nodded and left the office.

Houston had a metropolitan police department headed by a city sheriff. As Posey walked his horse from the courthouse back to Main Street, the sheriff and two of his uniformed officers approached him.

"I'm Sheriff Jess Monte. You look like a man in search of a hotel," Monte said.

"And a livery for my horse," Posey said.

"The Westerner is as good a hotel as any," Monte said. "Even has its own livery. I'll walk you over there."

"Obliged," Posey said.

The Westerner was a six-story structure with balconies on each room facing Main Street. A large livery stable was in the rear, and after checking in and bringing his rifles and gear into the lobby, a stable boy took care of Posey's horse.

"They serve a good steak here," Monte said.

"Join me for that steak around seven," Posey said.

"I'll do that," Monte said.

At the desk, Posey ordered a bath and was surprised when he was told his room had a tub, and a man would bring him hot water.

The fifth-floor room was large, well furnished, and the balcony overlooked the very busy Main Street. The tub was behind a door that led to a small private room. While the man brought in gallons of hot water, Posey shaved in front of the wall-mounted mirror.

"Well, I lived long enough," Posey said aloud, referencing the indoor tub Dale mentioned a while back.

"Excuse me, sir?" the man toting hot water said.

"Nothing. How do you get rid of the water when I'm done?" Posey asked the man.

"When you're finished, pull the plug at the bottom of the tub," the man said. "It's connected to a pipe that drains the water into a sewer underground."

"Where does the sewer go?" Posey said.

"I really don't know."

Posey gave the man a dollar and after he left, he slipped into the hot tub of water.

He thought about sending Dale a telegram, but other than worry his brother, what good would that do?

He stayed in the tub until the water cooled, then he pulled the plug and got out. As silly as it sounded, Posey stood naked over the tub and watched the water drain out of the tub until it was empty.

"I know Pepper Broussard only by reputation," Monte said. "And none of it is good."

Posey and Monte had just finished their steaks and were waiting for the waitress to clear the table.

"Let me ask you something. Why are you tracking this bunch alone?" Monte asked. "It seems like a job for an entire company."

"It would be if we knew his whereabouts," Posey said. "I'm just trying to get an idea where his hideout may be."

"It's not in Texas, I can tell you that much," Monte said.

"I'm going to see Judge Roy Bean," Posey said. "I understand he knows about Broussard."

"I never met Bean, but a lot of folks say he's just plumb crazy," Monte said. "My understanding is Broussard worked a few years as an enforcer for his so-called court."

The waitress came to the table.

"Will there be anything else?" she said.

"Do you have any ice cream?" Posey asked.

"Not this time of year," the waitress said. "We do have a good apple pie."

"Bring us the pie and coffee," Posey said.

The waitress nodded and walked away.

"Where exactly can I find the judge?" Posey asked.

"Follow the railroad construction south," Monte said.

CHAPTER TWENTY-ONE

After three days and nights in the saddle, Posey arrived in the territory known as Eagle's Nest, Texas, about twenty miles west of the Pecos River.

It was a dry, dusty place with just a few wood buildings, a blacksmith, a barn, and the Jersey Lilly Saloon, which also served as the courtroom for Judge Roy Bean.

The saloon was a good five miles from the railroad construction site, but judging from the horses tied out front, business was booming.

Posey tied his horse to the end of a long post and took the Sharps and Winchester with him when he entered the saloon.

About thirty railroad workers were drinking shots and beer. Roy Bean was holding court behind the bar, telling a story. He and everyone else fell silent as Posey walked to the bar.

Bean, close to sixty, was a thin man of

average height with a gray beard and hair. He wore an old Remington six-shooter in a worn holster. Everyone else in the bar was unarmed.

"I don't allow a man to go heeled in my courtroom," Bean said when Posey reached the bar.

"Your courtroom looks a lot like a saloon to me," Posey said and moved his vest to show his badge.

Bean looked at the badge.

"Is there a place we can talk?" Posey asked.

Bean turned to a skinny man wearing an apron who was also behind the bar.

"Chicken Foot, take over for a spell," Bean said. "And no free whiskey. And that means you too, Lard," Bean said to a wide barrel of a man at the end of the bar.

A porch behind the Jersey Lilly Saloon had a wood roof erected over it to provide relief from the Texas sun. Bean and Posey sat in chairs at a table that was basically a wood barrel with a wide, wood plank nailed to its top.

An unopened bottle of whiskey and two tin mugs rested between them. Bean opened the bottle and filled his cup nearly to the rim, then filled the second cup.

"A man needs to wet his whistle before talking business," Bean said.

He picked up his cup and drank half of it in several effortless swallows.

Posey picked up his cup and took a small swallow. "Now then, Judge," Posey said. "I need some information."

"Now hold on a minute there young fellow," Bean said and finished his cup of whiskey.

Posey pulled out his pouch and rolled a cigarette while Bean refilled his cup.

"Pepper Broussard," Posey said. "What can . . . ?"

Bean picked up his cup and swallowed half again and then set it down. "Now what is it you want?" he said.

"Pepper Broussard," Posey said. "What can you tell me about him?"

"He's a . . . roll me one of those, would you?"

Posey gave Bean the cigarette and rolled another. He struck a wood match and lit both cigarettes.

"Pepper Broussard you say," Bean said.

"I need to know everything you can tell me about him."

"As judge in these parts, I need to know why," Bean said.

"He's thrown in with an outlaw called

Tom Spooner, and he's wanted by the federal government," Posey said.

"Even west of the Pecos, I've heard of Tom Spooner," Bean said.

"About Broussard?"

"That one," Bean said. "A few years back I hired me a couple of enforcers, duly sworn in as justices of the peace. There's a lot of horse thieves, rustlers, and murderers about in these parts. I never seen nobody so quick as Broussard to kill a man when he didn't have to. I never even got the chance to hang those he went after on account he'd kill them first."

"I've heard he's good with a gun," Posey said.

"Best I've ever seen and I've seen 'em all from California to Texas," Bean said.

"Any idea how he hooked up with Spooner?"

Bean lifted his cup and chugged the remaining liquor until it was empty.

"Heard the expression water seeks its own level?" Bean said. "That's what I figure happened. They probably just found each other."

"When he worked for you, what kind of man was he?" Posey asked.

"Like I said, mean. Mean as they come, but that's what it takes to enforce the law in a place like this," Bean said. "If you find them, bring them to me. I won't waste time on locking them up. I'll hang them directly."

"Besides mean, anything else?" Posey asked.

"Anything else like what?"

"Does he gamble or drink too much? Spend all his time in whorehouses?"

"Never saw the man take more than one drink or play a hand of cards," Bean said. "The only whorehouse around here is a tent near the railroad. I can tell you this much: he'll draw down on a man faster than lightning from fifty feet or less. He's got weak eyes, you see. Any more than fifty feet, and he can't see a damn thing."

"Thanks for the information, Judge," Posey said. "I'll be sure to mention you in my report."

"Leaving so soon? Where are you headed?"

"Laredo."

"Laredo? That's a far piece from here."

"So I best get started," Posey said.

"Remember what I said. I'd hang them and save the federal government the expense," Bean said.

Posey rode an easy fifteen miles southeast toward Laredo. He knew what was coming and almost invited it to break up the monotony of the dry, dusty trail. He made camp at dusk, built a roaring fire near some tall, rocky hills, and then took care of his horse while beans and bacon cooked in a fry pan and coffee boiled.

Before he sat down to eat, Posey added whatever extra wood he could gather to the fire until it was an enormous blaze. Then he rested his back against the saddle and ate beans, bacon, and cornbread with a cup of coffee.

Finished eating, Posey spread out his bedroll and set his hat at one end. Then he took the Winchester rifle with him as he scaled the rocks and sat in the dark to wait.

Posey didn't have to wait long. He could hear horses approaching from a hundred yards away. As they closed in on his camp-site, Lard whispered, "I can smell his fire."

"Idiot, I can see his fire," Chicken Foot said. "Dismount. We'll walk in quiet-like and surprise him in the dark."

"Did you see that Colt he had?" Lard asked.

"We split his money and possibles, but that Colt is mine," Chicken Foot said.

"I got as much right to it as you," Lard said.

"No you don't neither," Chicken Foot said. "I saw it first. Now be quiet."

From his perch in the rocks, Posey watched as Chicken Foot and Lard slowly walked into his camp and stood beside the fire and looked at the bedroll. Both men carried rifles.

Posey cocked the lever of the Winchester.

Chicken Foot and Lard froze in place.

"Turn around slow," Posey said.

Chicken Foot and Lard turned and looked up at the dark hillside.

"You can't see me, but I can see you real clear standing beside that fire," Posey said. "Drop the rifles and gun belts."

Chicken Foot scanned the rocks.

Posey fired a shot at his feet and Chicken Foot jumped.

"I won't say it again," Posey said. "And if I do you won't live long enough to hear it."

Chicken Foot and Lard tossed their rifles and then dropped their gun belts.

"Now strip down to your underwear. Take off your boots, too," Posey said.

"I ain't taking off no . . ." Chicken Foot said.

Posey cocked and rapid-fired two shots at Chicken Foot's boots and said, "I won't tell you again."

"All right, mister, you win," Chicken Foot said.

Once they had stripped down to their

underwear, Lard said, "Now what?"

"Now you leave," Posey said. "You get on your horses and ride back to where you came from. If I see you again, I'll kill you both on sight."

"We'll meet again, you son of a bitch," Chicken Foot said.

"You better hope not," Posey said. "Go."

Once Chicken Foot and Lard returned to their horses and rode away, Posey came down from the rocks and extinguished the fire. He gathered up his belongings, saddled the horse, left Chicken Foot and Lard's weapons and clothes on the ground, and rode five miles in the dark before stopping for the night.

He didn't make a fire. There was no need. It was a warm night and the air was heavy. He rolled a cigarette and sat against his saddle while the horse grazed on what grass there was.

He thought about Tom Spooner.

About how good it would feel to kill him.

CHAPTER TWENTY-TWO

Laredo was a sprawling town of three thousand residents near the north bank of the Rio Grande River.

It was scorching hot and dust-dry when Posey rode into town close to eleven in the morning. Although the streets were crowded with people, no one seemed to be doing much of anything, and who could blame them in the heat of the day.

Posey walked his horse along the dusty streets and stopped in front of a wood structure with a sign on it that read Texas Rangers Law Enforcement. He hitched the horse to a post and stepped up to the wood plank sidewalk.

A dozen rangers were inside the building. A meeting was being conducted at a table by one man, and the group was huddled around the table. Every eye looked at Posey as he walked to the table.

"US Deputy Marshal Posey," Posey said.

"Bill McDonald," the man conducting the meeting said. "Captain, Texas Rangers."

"I seem to be disturbing your meeting," Posey said.

"We have a band of cattle rustlers east of here along the Rio Grande," McDonald said. "Stole Mexican beef. They crossed where the water level is low enough to traverse without drowning. The Mexican Federales chased them to the river, but they won't cross. They wired us, and we'll deal with them directly."

"Where can I cross the river into Mexico?" Posey asked.

"Probably where the rustlers crossed the cattle," McDonald said. "What's your business in Mexico?"

"Tracking an outlaw named Tom Spooner," Posey said.

"That one," McDonald said. "As far as I know, he's not set foot in Texas."

"Spooner's picked up a new traveling companion, a Texan named Pepper Broussard," Posey said.

"Now that one I'd hang on sight," McDonald said.

A ranger standing next to Posey said, "He brings to mind Bigfoot Wallace, this marshal does."

"I was thinking that very thing," Mc-

Donald said.

Bigfoot Wallace, a famous ranger who fought Santa Anna for the independence of Texas in eighteen thirty-six and rangered for thirty years or more, was a well-known figure throughout the country. Called Bigfoot for his enormous size and strength, he was a legend in Texas.

"We could use an extra hand if you care to join us, Marshal," McDonald said. "We'll be leaving right after the men get some chow and supplies. We don't expect to be back until morning."

"I need to cross anyway," Posey said. "Might as well."

The entire company plus Posey moved across the street to the Laredo Steak House, where they gorged on steaks. Posey sat with Captain McDonald and a few other rangers.

"Broussard is wanted in Texas for a dozen killings at least," McDonald said. "Not to mention horse stealing, cattle rustling, rape, and a host of other crimes."

"I understand he worked for Judge Roy Bean at one time," Posey said.

"That old buzzard should be hung himself," McDonald said.

"Broussard probably joined up with

Spooner to evade the law," Posey said.

"Could be," McDonald said. "We closed in on him a few times, but he always managed to evade us. Texas is a rather large place to hide out in. If he's joined up with Spooner, who knows where they are. Why you figure Mexico?"

"We got word he has some connections on the other side of the border," Posey said. "I need to check out the information."

"Well, you can find where the rustlers cross after we deal with them shortly," McDonald said.

It seemed as if half the town of Laredo turned out in the streets to watch the company of rangers mount up. Each of the twelve rangers stood by their horse and waited for Captain McDonald to give the order.

Posey stood beside his horse next to McDonald.

McDonald looked at his men. "Rangers, mount," he said.

The dozen rangers and Posey mounted their horses.

McDonald mounted his horse, gave the hand signal, and led the rangers and Posey out of town.

Some folks in the crowd even cheered.

■ ■ ■ ■

Ten miles northeast from Laredo, Mc-Donald held up the company and dismounted.

"Marshal, what do you make of this?" McDonald asked.

Posey dismounted and knelt beside McDonald. "Hundreds of tracks made by cattle and at least twenty horses rode north," McDonald said.

"What's north of here?" Posey asked.

"Looks like they're headed for the Pecos River," McDonald said. "They'll probably turn west into New Mexico from there."

Posey pressed his fingers into the deflated grass where the cattle had trodden it close to the ground. It was starting to spring back as trampled grass did when it grew.

"We won't catch them until morning," Posey said.

"Then we'll ride all night and catch them asleep at dawn," McDonald said. "Scout, you ride ahead and ride back if you see trouble," he said to a tall, thin ranger.

"I'll go with him," Posey said. "I did a fair amount of scouting for Sherman."

"Go," McDonald said. "The rest of us will follow."

"Build a fire so they can find us in the dark," Posey said. "Do you have a coffee pot and coffee?"

"I do," the scout said.

"I'll make two pots of coffee for the company," Posey said. "We'll need it if we're to ride until dawn."

"How far you figure we came?" the scout asked.

"Twenty mile, maybe a bit less," Posey said.

"About what I figure."

About an hour later, McDonald and the rangers arrived. "We'll rest an hour here," he said. "What do you think, Marshal? Can we catch them by dawn?"

"They're in no hurry, that's for sure," Posey said. "They haven't broke formation or changed direction once. It's the Pecos, all right. We can catch them."

"Everybody grab some coffee and eat what don't need cooking," McDonald said.

Posey, McDonald, and the company of rangers waited under the cover of predawn darkness for Scout to return on foot.

"I know we ain't federal like you boys, but

we could use a good man like yourself," Mc-Donald said to Posey.

"I have to finish my assignment first before I consider options," Posey said.

"Understandable," McDonald said.

"Here comes Scout," a ranger said.

Emerging from the twilight of darkness, Scout rode into the group of rangers.

"Captain, I counted fourteen," Scout said. "Two on watch, the others sleeping. A least a hundred head of Mexican beef, maybe a bit more. About a mile northwest, close to the Pecos."

"Every man check your six-shooter," Mc-Donald said. "We'll ride in hard and give any man who wants to surrender the opportunity to do so. Those that don't, shoot to kill. We ride in five minutes."

Posey removed his Colt from the holster and checked to make sure it was fully loaded and then returned it to the holster.

"Rangers, mount up," McDonald said.

Posey and the rangers mounted their horses.

"Draw guns," McDonald said. "Scout, lead the charge."

With Scout on the lead horse, the ranger company and Posey roared into the camp of the cattle thieves. By the time the two men on watch realized what was happening, Posey had shot one of them and Scout the other.

The remaining twelve rustlers, caught in their bedrolls, scattered, some with guns drawn. Others just ran.

Posey shot and killed four more by the time the shooting ended.

Three of the rustlers had surrendered and were on their knees. McDonald and the rangers dismounted, as did Posey.

"Count thirteen, Captain," Scout said.

"One is downwind," McDonald said.

One rustler had managed to escape by horse and was at least eight hundred yards to the north.

"Should we go after him, Captain?" Scout asked.

"Our horses ran all night," McDonald said. "His is fresh. We'll never catch him. Best let that one go, boys."

Posey withdrew the Sharps rifle from his saddle and inserted a massive .45-70 cartridge into the chamber and cocked it.

"What are you doing, Marshal?" McDonald asked. "He's way out of range."

Posey turned his horse and rested the enormous rifle over the saddle to steady it. He adjusted the rear sights and aimed carefully at the fading rider. Posey took a shallow breath, held it for a moment, and squeezed the trigger.

The noise of the shot was like a thunder-clap, and a full three seconds passed before the bullet struck the rider and he fell from his horse.

The rangers stared at Posey.

"That was some bully shot," McDonald said.

"What about the three prisoners, Captain?" Scout asked.

"I don't fancy dragging them all the way back to Laredo," McDonald said. "Find a good tree. We'll hang them here and save Laredo some tax dollars. If you find any identification, I'll wire their kin."

The ranger company had just four folding shovels and the men, including Posey, took turns digging graves. By late afternoon, all fourteen rustlers were buried in four large graves.

"We'll camp here and drive the herd to Laredo in the morning," McDonald said. "I'll wire the authorities in Mexico and tell them where to pick up their beef."

Several fires were built, hot food cooked, and coffee boiled, and the company gathered around the fires to eat.

"Marshal, that shot you made today must have been nine hundred yards," McDonald said. "You've got a hell of an eye. My company sure could use you. I hope when your business is concluded you'll come see me."

"I might just do that, but I'll need to cross the river in the morning," Posey said.

"Scout will track the crossing point for you, Marshal," McDonald said.

"Obliged," Posey said.

"Are you a drinking man, Marshal?" McDonald asked.

"On occasion," Posey said.

McDonald removed a silver flask from a pocket of his jacket and twisted off the cap. "Join me in a sip," he said and took a swallow.

Posey took the flask and had a sip. It was rye whiskey. He gave the flask back to McDonald and pulled out his tobacco pouch.

"Save that," McDonald said. "Have one of these."

McDonald had a silver cigar holder that held six cigars. He removed the lid and pulled out two cigars. "Come all the way from the island of Cuba south of Florida," he said.

Posey took the cigar. "Obliged," he said and struck a match.

"Hey, Scout, bring us two cups of coffee," McDonald said.

Scout filled two cups with coffee and brought them to McDonald. "Here you go, Captain," he said.

McDonald added an ounce of rye whiskey to each cup and passed one to Posey.

"Are you a church-going man?" McDonald asked.

"On occasion," Posey said.

"I'm an ordained minister myself," McDonald said. "I hold services every Sunday at the church in Laredo. I insist all my men attend. Sometimes we have a picnic and games for the children after the service. The girls jump rope and the boys play that game where you hit a ball with a stick."

"Baseball," Posey said.

"That's it," McDonald said. "Mind a question? What did you do for Sherman in the war?"

"Advanced scout, some snipering when required," Posey said. "I once made a shot from eleven hundred yards."

"I've been a ranger since 'fifty-nine," McDonald said. "When the war broke out, I decided my duty was more necessary in Texas, so I missed the fighting. Were you on the march to the sea?"

"I was."

"I read how horrific it was," McDonald said.

"I don't believe there is a word in the English language to describe the things we did on that march," Posey said. "They called it war. We burned the entire city of Atlanta and many raped and killed women and livestock, robbed and looted, and even killed children. I don't know what you would call it, but I'm sure of one thing: it wasn't war, and the word 'horrific' falls far short in description."

McDonald stared at Posey.

"I believe I'll turn in and get an early start in the morning," Posey said.

After breakfast, Posey and McDonald shook hands.

"Marshal, it's been a pleasure riding with you," McDonald said.

"Same here," Posey said.

"Hope to see you again," McDonald said. "Scout, see if you can find that crossing for the marshal."

Posey and Scout watched the company of rangers mount up and slowly drive the herd of stolen cattle to Laredo.

"Well," Scout said. "Let's see if we can find that river crossing."

By noon, Scout had tracked the path of the herd close to the Rio Grande River.

"The tracks turn southwest a bit here," he said. "Let's give the horses an hour's rest. I'll make a fire and boil us some coffee."

Once the coffee was ready, Posey brought out a one-pound loaf of cornbread, broke off a hunk, and gave it to Scout.

"I do love cornbread," Scout said as he dunked it in his cup.

"How far across the river is Nuevo?" Posey asked.

"Depends where you cross," Scout said. "I'll be able to tell when we find the spot."

"Here," Scout said. "They crossed here."

Posey and Scout dismounted and inspected the site where the cattle had crossed.

"The silt is up right now," Scout said. "Makes for easy crossing. Can't be more than a few hundred yards."

"Nuevo?" Posey asked.

Scout pointed southeast. "Fifteen mile that way."

"Thanks."

"Wait," Scout said. "Captain asked me to give you this."

Scout dug a silver pocket watch and chain from a pocket and held it out to Posey. The badge of the Texas Rangers was embossed on the watch cover.

"He noticed you didn't have a watch," Scout said.

"I . . . lost it on the trail somewhere," Posey said as he took the watch.

"Best of luck to you," Scout said and mounted his horse.

Posey watched Scout ride away and when he was in the distance, he rolled a cigarette and found a rock to sit on and smoke it.

He looked at the watch. It was made of pure silver, and the badge of the Texas Rangers was embossed on the cover plate. Even the chain was pure silver. He pressed the winder button and the cover plate opened. The face of the watch showed the badge of the Rangers painted on a white background with an hour, minute, and second hand in black.

It must have cost fifty dollars or more to make such a timepiece.

Posey closed the faceplate, attached the chain to his belt, and stuck the watch into his right front pocket.

He looked across the Rio Grande at Old Mexico.

"Damn," he said aloud and then went to his horse and mounted the saddle. "Let's get our feet wet."

Chapter Twenty-Three

After crossing the Grande, Posey rode southeast for a dozen or so easy miles. By his new pocket watch, the time was a few minutes before the hour of two. He stopped for a bit to give the horse a rest and to eat some cornbread.

The Mexican sun was hot, and the back of his shirt stuck to his skin. He drank some water from his canteen and then poured a little over his hair and face.

Before mounting the saddle, he checked the placement of the sun for direction and then kept on a southeastern path.

The Mexican scenery wasn't much different from that of Texas. If not for the Rio Grande dividing the two countries, the land was one and the same.

After a few more miles, Posey rode right into a cornfield. Acres and acres of cornstalks, six feet high. He dismounted and inspected the corn. It was close to harvest.

He was about to mount up when the screams of a woman shattered the silence of the cornfield.

The woman was screaming in Spanish.

Posey left the horse and followed the sounds of her screams. As he neared the source, he drew the Colt and cocked it.

The screams silenced.

Loud rustling in the cornfield caught his attention and Posey followed the sound.

At the edge of the field, four horses grazed on tall grass. Cornstalks rustled loudly. A man's voice said, "Hold her still, damn you."

Another man said, "What about us?"

"You'll all get a turn, now hold her still, damn you."

Posey turned at the edge of the field.

Two men stood with their backs to him. Another man knelt in front of a naked woman. A fourth man held the woman's arms stretched out over her head.

The man holding the woman's arms said, "She's a hellcat, this one. I see what Tom likes about her."

The man kneeling opened his pants. "Never mind Tom and hold her steady," he said and punched the woman in the face.

The man holding the woman's arms noticed Posey, released her arms, and stood up. "Company," he said.

The two men with their backs to Posey spun around and reached for their guns and Posey shot them in the chest.

The man kneeling in front of the woman turned, and Posey shot him once in the chest and a second time in the face.

Posey looked at the remaining man.

"You going to just look at me or skin that smoke wagon?" Posey said quietly as he holstered the Colt.

The man's eyes told Posey he was scared to death.

"Make your move, boy," Posey said. "I saw what you can do against a woman. Let's see what you can do against someone a little bigger."

The man stood motionless.

"No?" Posey said. "Maybe you'd like it if I was naked and tied down?"

The man reached for his gun and before he even touched it, Posey shot him twice.

The first two men weren't dead. Posey opened the loading gate of the Colt, removed the six spent cartridges, and reloaded. Then he stood over the two men still drawing breath and ended their breathing with two well-placed shots.

Posey holstered the Colt and went to the woman. She was unconscious. She was Mexican and beautiful to look at, for sure.

The right side of her face was red and swollen from the punch, and blood leaked from her nose and lip.

Her clothes were ripped to shreds and useless.

Posey lifted her in his arms and carried her to his horse. He set her down gently, removed the blanket from his bedroll, wrapped her in it, and then placed her in the saddle. He mounted the saddle behind her and gave the reins a soft tug.

Nuevo wasn't much of a town to look at. Some adobe buildings, a church, a round fountain filled with water and topped with the statue of the Virgin Mary, and a small mill powered by a donkey.

Farmers and their women came out of hiding when Posey rode into the town square with the woman on his horse. He stopped at the fountain.

"Does anybody speak English?" Posey said.

A farmer dressed in typical Mexican work clothes stepped forward. *"Sí,"* he said.

"*Sí* is Spanish," Posey said.

"Yes, I speak English," the man said.

"This woman is hurt," Posey said and dismounted and took the woman in his arms.

"Bring her into the church," the man said.

Posey smoked a cigarette as he sat on the stone fountain. It was filled with water, and he dipped his bandanna in it and wiped his face.

Some men and women watched him from a distance.

The man who spoke English came out of the church and walked to him.

"She isn't hurt badly," he said. "What happened to her clothes?"

"Four men tried to rape her in your cornfield," Posey said.

The man nodded. "Tom Spooner's men," he said. "Spooner will kill them for that."

"I already did it for him," Posey said.

The man looked at Posey's badge. "You are from America?"

"What's your name?" Posey asked.

"Joseph."

"Well, Joseph, how did you know those were Spooner's men?"

"He sends men sometimes when he needs a place to hide," Joseph said. "He must be planning another robbery close to the border."

"And they were here, the men I killed?"

"Yes. This morning. They took some supplies and rode out."

"Most of your people live on farms?"

"All around us," Joseph said.

"That woman live on a farm?"

"It was probably her cornfield you found her in."

"So they rode to her farmhouse and took her," Posey said. "Does she live alone?"

"With her father and two younger brothers," Joseph said. "I sent someone to fetch them. Their farm is several miles from here. They have mules but no horses."

Posey looked at the adobe church.

"Where's your *padre*?"

"He . . . got in the way of Spooner," Joseph said. "He is buried behind the church."

Posey tossed his cigarette into the dirt. "I came here looking for Pilar Lobos," he said. "Do you know where I can find her?"

"You can find her in the church wrapped in your blanket," Joseph said.

Posey stood up and Joseph said, "The women won't allow you in until they've attended to her," he said.

An old man suddenly came rushing past and ran to the church.

"Her father," Joseph said. "There is nothing you can do at the moment. Come into the cantina and have something to eat and drink."

■ ■ ■ ■

The interior of the cantina was lit by dozens of candles placed on tables. Joseph sat with Posey at a table by a window. Several men were gathered at tables, and they spoke in hushed tones.

Posey was served a plate of rice and beans with shredded beef, flat bread, and tequila.

"Have you had tequila before, Marshal?" Joseph asked.

"Can't say as I have," Posey said.

"I don't think you can find it in the states," Joseph said. "It is made from the agave plant, but you must sip it slowly."

Posey took a small sip. "Not unlike mezcal, but smoother and sweeter," he said.

"Why are you looking for Pilar?" Joseph asked.

"I'm hunting Spooner and his gang," Posey said. "Talk is Spooner is sweet on her. I want to talk to her, is all."

"Go ahead," Joseph said and looked at the door.

Wearing men's pants, shirt, and slippers of some kind, Pilar stood in the doorway and searched for Posey. The right side of her face was still swollen and bruised, as was her upper lip.

She spotted him at the table and walked to him.

"You are the American marshal that saved me?" she said. She had a slight accent, but her English was close to perfect.

Posey nodded.

"Joseph, leave us," Pilar said.

Joseph stood up and walked to a table where some men were drinking.

Pilar grabbed a shot glass from another table, filled it with tequila, and downed it in one quick gulp.

Then she sat. "I am Pilar Lobos," she said.

"I know."

"How did you happen by my cornfield?" she asked as she refilled her glass with tequila.

"I'm tracking Tom Spooner," Posey said. "I heard you know him."

"Yes, I know him," Pilar said.

"What can you tell me about him?"

"I can tell you he is a filthy pig of a man who should be hung by the neck until dead," Pilar said.

"Besides that."

"Did you kill the men who attacked me?"

"Yes."

"Good."

"How did they happen to grab you?"

"They came to town yesterday and stayed

overnight," Pilar said. "Spooner must be planning a robbery near the border. He comes here to hide from the law if he's close to the border. Those men must have been his scouts timing the ride across the border. When they don't return, he will send more."

"And they grabbed you on the way out?"

"I was inspecting the corn," Pilar said. "They rode by, and you know the rest."

Posey nodded. He looked across the cantina at Joseph. "Joseph, a moment," he said.

Joseph came to the table.

"Take as many men as you can gather and shovels and go bury those men," Posey said. "Bury them with their saddles and weapons. If they have money, keep it. Set the horses free, but take them off a good distance before you do that. Go now, quickly."

Joseph nodded. "Right away, Marshal."

After Joseph left the cantina, Pilar said, "The people here could use those horses."

"And when Spooner sends more men and they see those horses but not the men, they will most likely burn your town down and kill innocent people," Posey said.

Pilar nodded. "Yes, of course."

"I'd like to know everything you . . ." Posey said.

Pilar's father entered the cantina and

spoke angrily at Pilar in Spanish. Pilar responded in Spanish and stood up.

"My father wants me to go home and rest," Pilar said. "We have supper at eight o'clock. I would like you to join us. We can talk more about Tom Spooner then. Ride two miles to the east and past my cornfield by about a mile."

Posey nodded. "All right."

After Pilar and her father left the cantina, Posey went outside where Joseph had gathered eight men. Each man had a shovel. Posey went to his horse and removed the folding shovel from his gear.

"I'll go with you," Posey told Joseph.

Posey chose a site on the north side of the cornfield where the graves wouldn't be seen by riders passing by. He and the men dug two very deep graves and buried Spooner's men with their saddles.

Before burying them, Posey went through their pockets and saddlebags and collected one hundred and forty dollars in gold coins and folding money and gave it to Joseph.

It was late afternoon by the time the chore was done.

"Joseph, take the reins of a horse and have two of your men do the same," Posey said.

"We'll walk the horses a piece and release them."

They walked about a mile north to a field of open grass and Posey removed the bit and reins from the four horses and tossed them away.

"They'll be fine," Posey said. "Send your men ahead, and let's you and me have a talk."

Joseph spoke to his men in Spanish and they set off on foot.

Posey and Joseph sat in the shade of a tree and Posey rolled a cigarette.

"When Spooner and his bunch ride in, why doesn't someone send for the law?" Posey asked.

"We never know when he is going to show up," Joseph said. "And the nearest federal police is forty miles to the south, and we have no horses. Even if we did have one, Spooner would kill the man riding it and probably the horse, too."

"I understand," Posey said. "Tell me what you can about Spooner."

"He is a big man like you," Joseph said. "And has no regard for life. If we don't obey him when he is here, he will destroy our village and burn the crops. So we do as he says until he leaves."

"How long does he stay when he shows up?"

"Sometimes a week, sometimes less."

"Can you remember the times when he was here?" Posey asked. "The months or weeks and how long he stayed."

"Late March or early April, and the time before that was January," Joseph said. "Before that was November last. After that, I can't remember the month."

"Thank you, Joseph," Posey said. "Let's go back to town."

The small village was coming to life when Posey and Joseph returned as late afternoon gave way to early evening.

"Joseph, is there someplace I can wash and change my shirt?" Posey asked. "I will be having supper with Pilar and her family."

"In back of the cantina," Joseph said. "I will have them bring you fresh water to shave and wash."

"Thank you, Joseph."

Posey shaved, washed, and changed his shirt. He retrieved his horse from the hitching post at the cantina and found Joseph talking with some men at the fountain.

"Is there a place I can sleep tonight?" Posey asked Joseph.

"There is a room behind the cantina," Jo-

seph said. "It will be ready when you return."

"Thank you, Joseph," Posey said and rode
east.

CHAPTER TWENTY-FOUR

Posey arrived at Pilar's farmhouse near dusk. It was a two-story cabin that must have taken years to construct. A wide porch and railing dominated the front of the house. It was more in the style of a house you saw in Texas than in Mexico. A corral with two mules stood to the left near a wide barn.

Lanterns glowed in the windows.

Posey dismounted and tied his horse to the corral. Pilar was waiting for him on the porch. She was seated in a rocking chair and stood when he came up the steps.

Her dark hair hung loose, down around her shoulders. She wore a simple black dress that had lace around the neckline with plain shoes, yet she appeared beautiful and elegant despite the swollen bruise.

"Please come inside and meet my brothers and father," Pilar said.

Pilar opened the screen door and Posey

followed her into the house. The interior was rustic and simple, not unlike a thousand such homes Posey saw scattered across the American plains. The furniture appeared all homemade. A stone fireplace was centered in the living room.

"We take our meals in the kitchen," Pilar said.

Pilar led Posey into the kitchen where her father and two brothers sat at a long wood table.

"The tall one is Roberto," Pilar said. "He is eighteen. Call him Robert. The small one is Carlos. He is fourteen. Call him Charlie."

Posey removed his hat and nodded. "Robert and Charlie it is," he said.

"They speak English as well," Pilar said. "I taught them both when they were children."

Pilar walked to her father and stood behind his chair.

"May I present my father, Jose Lorenzo Lobos," Pilar said. "He also speaks English very well, although it annoys him to do so."

"I apologize, Mr. Lobos, my Spanish is very poor," Posey said.

"I will speak English to the man who saved my daughter's honor and her life," Jose said. "Please sit at my table."

"Thank you, sir," Posey said.

Posey took one of two vacant chairs at the table.

Pilar went to the woodstove and began to serve the meal of rice and beans with corn, beef with flat bread, and wine for the adults, milk for Robert and Charlie. Then she took the chair next to Posey.

Jose bowed his head and recited grace in Spanish and then English.

"Please forgive my inquisitive nature, Marshal, but when it concerns my daughter I must ask," Jose said. "Did you kill those men before they violated her?"

"Papa, that is no question for the dinner table," Pilar said.

Posey noticed her skin flushed and her eyes darkened when she was angry.

"You were unconscious, so how would you know?" Jose said to Pilar.

"Mr. Lobos, rest assured, I killed them before they got the chance," Posey said.

Jose nodded. "I am grateful to God for that," he said.

"I wish I was there," Robert said. "I would have stopped them."

"Me, too," Charlie said.

"They would have killed the both of you little mice," Pilar said. "Now, no more talk of killing while we eat."

"Marshal, try the wine," Jose said. "It is quite good."

"It is Mexican coffee," Pilar said. "Very strong. I added some sugar and condensed milk."

They were seated in chairs on the front porch after supper.

Posey sampled the coffee. "It's very good."

"It occurred to me that I haven't thanked you for saving my life," Pilar said.

"I think dinner did that," Posey said. He pulled out his tobacco pouch and looked at Pilar. "Do you mind?"

"No, go ahead."

Posey rolled a cigarette and lit it with a wood match.

"Tom Spooner has managed to evade the law for many years, even though lawmen across the country are hunting him," Posey said. "I figure he has a secret place he uses as a hideout. I was told that he is sweet on you and crosses the border to see you. That's why I was riding past your cornfield this morning, to see you."

Pilar sipped coffee and then smiled softly at Posey. "And you saw a lot more of me than you expected to see," she said.

Posey felt himself grin. "I did my best not to look when I covered you in my blanket."

"I don't believe you, but thank you for saying it," Pilar said.

"So what can you tell me?" Posey asked.

"Several years ago, Spooner and his men showed up after they robbed a bank in Texas," Pilar said. "They were running from the law, crossed the river, and found Nuevo by accident. We are a poor village without protection, and they stayed and took what they wanted and did what they wanted. I was in the town square that day and Spooner saw me. I was married but one week. His name was Tomas Escalante and he was a good man. His family has a farm south of the village. You met his father. His name is Joseph."

Posey closed his eyes for a moment. "Yes," he said. "What happened to Tomas?"

"Spooner grabbed me in the town square and Tomas hit him," Pilar said. "Spooner shot him three times in the chest. We buried him on Joseph's farm. The next day, Spooner and his men left."

"How many men?"

"Sometimes twenty, sometimes more."

"When he came back the next time, what happened?"

"It was months later," Pilar said. "They returned, and Spooner said I was to be his woman or he would kill everybody in the village and burn it down."

Pilar sipped from her cup and then made eye contact with Posey. "I figured it was better to have him put his hands on me than murder innocent people."

Posey nodded.

"Has he ever sent scouts to the village before?"

"Yes. I believe when he is going to rob a bank near the border, he will come here to hide for a while," Pilar said. "Sometimes I hear his men talking."

"When those men I killed don't return, he will send more to find out what happened," Posey said.

"I know," Pilar said.

"Would you have any idea where Spooner's hideout might be?" Posey asked. "Even a general location or area."

"I've heard them speak of Wyoming," Pilar said.

"Wyoming's a big territory," Posey said.

"It's all I know," Pilar said.

"Well, it's more than I knew this morning."

"Wait, you just can't ride away in the morning," Pilar said. "He will send more men when those four don't return. You said that yourself. They will murder innocent people and burn the village."

"It could take days for them to show up," Posey said. "Wyoming is . . ."

"Wyoming isn't going anyplace," Pilar said angrily. "It will still be there in another week or so. Yes?"

Posey looked at Pilar's coal-black eyes, which blazed with anger, and he sighed. "Yes."

"We will hold a village meeting in the morning," Pilar said, her eyes softening.

"After breakfast, I hope?" Posey said.

"Yes, of course," Pilar said.

"Well, I best get to town," Posey said. "Joseph said I could sleep in the room behind the cantina."

"People meet at seven in the square to use the mill," Pilar said. "The cantina serves breakfast at seven-thirty. I will be there at eight to start the meeting."

Posey stood up and said, "Then I'll see you in the morning."

He left the porch and walked to the corral where he mounted his horse. Before riding away, Posey looked back at the porch. Pilar was standing, watching him in the light of a wall-mounted lantern.

Framed by the soft, flickering light, she looked beautiful.

CHAPTER TWENTY-FIVE

Posey awoke around six-thirty to find a fresh basin of water with a towel waiting for him right outside the door. As he washed his face, he could hear people speaking Spanish in front of the cantina.

He didn't have a clean shirt and wore the one from the day before. After holstering his Colt, Posey went to the front of the cantina. A dozen or more farmers were at the mill where the mule powered the grinding stone by walking a harness attached to a long log in a tight circle.

Mule-driven carts of corn and wheat were lined up at the mill.

Joseph broke away from the group and approached Posey.

"Marshal, come into the cantina and have some breakfast," Joseph said.

Posey followed Joseph into the cantina. Every table was occupied except one.

"Please sit. I told them to hold a table for

you," Joseph said.

"Will you join me in breakfast?" Posey said. "I hate to eat alone."

"Thank you, Marshal, I will," Joseph said.

A woman came to the table and Joseph spoke to her in Spanish. She nodded and went into the kitchen.

"The town square is always like this on days when the mill is used," Joseph said. "They come from miles around and it's an all-day event."

"I heard about you son," Posey said. "I'm sorry to hear that."

"One day Spooner will pay for his crimes," Joseph said. "In this life or the next."

The woman returned with two large mugs of coffee.

"I told her to add sugar and condensed milk," Joseph said.

Posey nodded and took a sip. "Do you have other children, a wife?" he asked.

"I have three other sons," Joseph said. "They will be men soon. My wife died three years ago from . . . what is the word. Disease of the lung."

"Tuberculosis?"

"Yes, tuberculosis," Joseph said.

"You have a hard life down here," Posey said.

"Yes hard, but also a good life," Joseph

said. "People in our village care for each other and we share in the crops and livestock. We lack for nothing to live on that our land doesn't supply."

"How is it you speak English so well?" Posey asked.

"I was born in Texas when it was still part of Mexico," Joseph said. "I was a small boy, but I learned English in school as well as Spanish. My family moved across the Grande in 'forty-five because they didn't want to live in Texas anymore after it became a state. They moved us here, and here we stayed."

The woman returned with a large tray of food. Scrambled eggs with rice and beans, flat bread, and a bottle of hot sauce.

"The sauce is very hot, so just use a little," Joseph said.

Posey sprinkled a bit of sauce on his eggs, rice, and beans and then tasted it. "Yes it is, but good," he said.

"Eat," Joseph said.

Posey dug in and said, "Pilar is coming to town at eight this morning. She wants to have a village meeting. Will you act as my translator?"

"I will," Joseph said.

"Good."

■ ■ ■ ■

A few minutes before eight, Posey stood in front of the cantina with a cup of coffee and a cigarette. There was much arguing and laughter among the men. Women worked to unload carts and fill woven baskets with milled grain.

Walking, Pilar arrived at the town square. She wore black pants, a white shirt, black boots, and a black Stetson hat. The bruise on her face was barely noticeable. She spotted Posey and walked to him.

"Good morning, Marshal," she said.

"Morning," Posey said. "I see you're a quick healer."

Pilar touched her cheek. "It's amazing what a bit of face powder can do."

"How many of these people speak English?"

"Some. Not many."

"Get their attention," Posey said. "I've asked Joseph to translate for me."

Pilar nodded and then walked to the fountain and stood on the wall. She spoke loudly in Spanish, and slowly the men and women around the mill stopped what they were doing and migrated to the fountain.

Posey walked to the crowd and looked at Joseph.

"Translate for me," Posey said.

"I'm United States Marshal Jack Posey and, as some of you know, I killed four of the outlaw Tom Spooner's men yesterday," Posey said and Joseph translated. "I believe that when those four men don't return to the outlaw Spooner, he will send more to find out what happened to them."

After Joseph translated, the crowd began to buzz and speak wildly.

"Please, please, allow me to finish," Posey said.

Joseph translated and they quieted down.

"I am willing to stay and help when the new men arrive, but you must listen to me and do as I ask," Posey said.

Joseph translated and the crowd responded by speaking rapidly at him.

To Posey, Joseph said, "They want to know how you will help."

"Tell them that when Spooner's men show up, I will kill them," Posey said. "And that after these men are dead, I believe Spooner will send no more men."

As Joseph translated, Pilar walked to Posey and stood next to him.

"They want to know how you will do this and how can they help?" Joseph said.

"Tell them I will let them know," Posey said.

Joseph translated and then walked to Posey.

Posey said, "Let's go in the cantina and have a cup of coffee."

Posey took a sip of coffee and then said, "Joseph, does anybody in the village have guns?"

"Guns? Some of us have rifles," Joseph said.

"Good. Pilar, how far would you say it is from your cornfield to the center of the village?" Posey asked.

"Two miles, maybe a bit more."

"When Spooner's men ride across the border, do they always pass your field?"

"It's the shortest route," Pilar said.

"We need to find out the time it takes to ride a horse at a normal pace from your field to the village," Posey said.

"Why?" Pilar asked.

"Because they won't be traveling on foot," Posey said. "Joseph, gather together your guns and meet us at the town square when Pilar and I return."

"Return from where?" Pilar said.

From the saddle, Posey reached down and

took hold of Pilar's right hand and pulled her up behind him.

Then he pulled out his pocket watch, gave the stem a few turns to wind it, checked the time, and put it away.

He gave the reins a tug and the horse moved forward.

"They might be in a bit of a hurry, but I doubt they will be running flat out," Posey said.

Pilar wrapped her arms around Posey's waist. The man was all solid muscle. "I don't see what that matters," she said.

"Like in war, surprise and timing is everything," Posey said.

Traveling at a medium speed, they arrived at Pilar's cornfield in about fifteen minutes.

Posey turned the horse and headed to Pilar's home.

"Why are we going to my home?" she asked.

"I need to speak with your family," Posey said.

"Yes, I can do that," Jose said.

"We can help," Robert said.

"Yes, Papa, we can help." Charlie echoed his brother.

They were on the porch of Pilar's farmhouse.

"And while I am waiting in the cornfield, who is doing all the work on the farm?" Jose said.

"Do you have a watch?" Posey asked.

"Yes," Jose said.

"Make sure you wait seven and a half minutes," Posey said.

Jose nodded. "I will be there before dawn," he said.

"Good."

"What about me?" Pilar said.

"You stay here with your brothers," Posey said.

"Spooner's men don't frighten me," Pilar said.

"Maybe not, but bullets should," Posey said.

Pilar glared at Posey as he stepped off the porch and mounted his horse.

"By the way, Mr. Lobos, do you have a gun?" Posey asked.

"No, not for a long time now," Jose said.

"Well, you shouldn't need one," Posey said and gave the reins a yank.

Posey met Joseph in the town square.

"I have the rifles inside the cantina," Joseph said.

"Lead the way," Posey said.

In a storeroom behind the kitchen, eleven

Civil War muskets were stacked neatly against the wall.

Posey lifted one and inspected it.

"Joseph, these are Civil War muskets," he said. "The hammers and triggers are rusted solid. They're useless."

"It's just as well, as we have no powder and balls," Joseph said.

"It doesn't matter," Posey said. "Let's have some coffee, and I'll tell you what I need you to do."

They went inside to a table and Joseph ordered two cups of coffee.

"When I give the signal, you take everybody who happens to be in the town square, at the mill, the cantina, and everywhere else, and lock them inside the church," Posey said. "The windows and door are wood and will burn, but those adobe walls are near fireproof. Does it lock from the inside?"

"Yes, and the windows, too."

"Good. Have you a ladder?"

In the cramped bedroom behind the cantina, Posey sat in the lone chair at the small table by the window and cleaned his guns. First the Sharps rifle, which was the easiest to break down.

Part of the supplies he picked up in Laredo were two cleaning kits, one for the rifles and another for the Colt.

With a long wire brush, Posey cleaned the barrel of the Sharps until it was spotless. Then he wiped and lightly oiled all moving parts before reassembling the rifle. He repeated the process with the Winchester.

In the cleaning kit for the Colt were tiny tools that he used to remove the screws and carefully take apart the frame and inner workings. With the wire brush, Posey cleaned the bore, then wiped and lightly oiled all the parts.

Once the Colt was reassembled, he loaded six fresh cartridges into the wheel and closed the gate.

"Marshal Posey, are you in there?" Pilar said from outside the room.

Posey holstered the Colt and stepped outside.

"I've come to speak with you," Pilar said.

"Go ahead."

"When do you expect Spooner's men to arrive?"

"Tomorrow," Posey said. "If I were him and the first four didn't return, that's all the time I'd give them. Then I'd dispatch more men to find out what happened."

"And when they arrive?"

"I will kill them," Posey said.

Pilar stared at Posey.

"Do you object?" Posey asked.

Pilar slowly shook her head.

"I want to help," she said.

"Out of the question," Posey said.

"I live in this village and I am free to go where I please," Pilar said.

"Tomorrow you're not," Posey said.

"Let me ask you something Marshal Posey . . . and by the way, what is your first name?"

"My Christian name is John, but I've been called Jack since I was a pup."

"Okay, Marshal Jack Posey, when Spooner's men ride into the village, what is your plan? There will be people in the square, at the mill and cantina."

"Joseph will bring everybody into the church and lock it from the inside," Posey said.

"And leave you alone in the streets?"

"I can't do what I need to do if I have to worry about you," Posey said.

"I'm a grown woman, twenty-seven years old. You do not need to worry about me," Pilar said.

Posey sighed.

"Don't sigh. Little boys sigh."

"Maybe you could help Joseph get people into the church," Posey said.

"I could do that."

"But you go in with them and lock the doors."

"I could do that."

"Can you be in the town square by dawn?"

"Yes."

"You'll go in the church when I say so."

"I said I would."

"All right then."

"Can you give me a ride back to the farm?" Pilar said.

"I'll get my horse."

Pilar wrapped her arms around Posey's stomach and said, "Can't this horse go any faster?"

"Of course he can," Posey said.

"Then make him go faster," Pilar said. "My father and brothers will be coming in from the field and will expect supper."

Posey gave the reins a yank and the massive horse opened his stride.

Pilar held on tight and said, "Better."

"My cart is full of straw," Jose said. "All I need to do in the morning is hitch the mule."

"You made a tall circle of rocks so the fire doesn't spread?" Posey asked.

"It took all afternoon, but we did," Jose said.

"Good. Once you set the fire, you get in your cart and ride back here as fast as you can. Understand?"

"Yes."

Pilar came out to the porch. "Will you be staying for supper, Marshal Posey?"

"Yes, stay," Jose said. "I insist."

Riding back to the village after dark, Posey felt an odd sensation. He knew it was in his mind, but as he rode, he could still feel Pilar's arms wrapped around his stomach and felt the warmth of her touch against his skin.

It was a foreign sensation to him.

A feeling he had no words for.

He had always liked women, but never thought about one before once she was out of his sight.

Pilar's arms around his waist sent a chill down his spine the likes he hadn't felt since combat in the war. It was like a sudden surge of unexpected excitement.

The funny part was that she probably had no idea of the sensation she caused him with just a simple touch.

"Jack Posey, you're nothing but a big dope," he said aloud as he entered the village.

CHAPTER TWENTY-SIX

Shortly after dawn, Posey took his Winchester rifle and climbed the ladder behind the church to the roof. From a height of twenty feet, he had a clear, unobstructed view for miles.

He took out his pocket watch, gave it a few winds, and set it on the ledge where he could see it.

He rolled a cigarette and smoked while he watched Pilar walk into the village. She wore blue wrangler pants that hugged her hips, and a black shirt with buttons that did justice to her well-shaped upper body. She wore the Stetson hat to shield the sun and cowboy boots.

She didn't look up as she met Joseph at the mill where they chatted for a while.

He heard footsteps on the ladder, and a woman from the cantina appeared with a plate of food and a cup of coffee.

"I brought you breakfast, Marshal," she

said in a thick accent.

He took the plate and cup. "Thank you. I appreciate it," Posey said.

He ate as he watched the horizon.

At the mill, farmers went about their business. Wheat was being ground today, carts full of the grain.

Missing was the chatter and sound of laughter.

Even from the height of the church rooftop, he could see the sense of fear and doom on the townspeople's faces.

Jose sat in his cart and waited.

The time passed slowly. He had much to think about. A father knows his children, Jose thought. Their different personalities, their likes and dislikes, and even their quirks. Carlos was in a hurry to become a man. He would learn one day that the best time of a man's life is spent in youth. Roberto had the wanderlust, and Jose knew it wouldn't be too long before he left the farm in search of adventure. Someday he would learn that adventure begins in a man's heart and not his location.

Pilar was a woman of the highest regard. She worked the fields with him until her hands bled. As honorable as Tomas was, Jose knew Pilar didn't love him, and only married him because the Escalante farm was twice the size of his and would assure her family wealth in bad times.

She . . . sacrificed her honor by allowing Tom Spooner to lay hands upon her to save the lives of her family, friends, and the village.

And she never complained. She had the spirit of a wild mustang and the heart of a mountain lion.

She could go to America, to Texas or New Mexico, and live a good life, a much easier life, but she would never leave her father and brothers as long as men like Tom Spooner threatened the very existence of the village.

Jose had never seen his daughter in love before. Women wore their love like the bloom of a rose for all to see, if you knew enough to look. He saw that bloom on her face whenever she was in the company of the marshal.

The marshal would leave when his job was done and . . .

Four riders suddenly passed the cornfield. They couldn't see the cart for the high cornstalks a hundred yards deep. Jose opened his pocket watch and checked the time. It was just a few minutes past nine. The riders were in no hurry, as the marshal had predicted.

Jose waited in the cart for seven and one half minutes. When he climbed down, he could no longer see the four riders. He went to the circle of stones he and his sons built yesterday. He dug out a match, struck it against the stone, and set fire to the hay inside the circle.

As the hay caught fire, Jose made the sign of the cross and then returned to his cart.

Posey was sipping coffee when he spotted the faint smoke rising in the sky far in the distance. He looked at his watch on the ledge. Twelve minutes past nine.

Joseph was talking to some people at the mill.

"Joseph, get everybody into the church," Posey yelled. "Now!"

Joseph looked up at Posey.

"Now, Joseph," Posey hollered.

Joseph started speaking in Spanish and directing people into the church. Within minutes, the streets of the village were deserted.

Posey watched the distance, and four dots appeared on the horizon. He didn't need binoculars to know they were four of Spooner's men advancing toward the village. He looked at the watch again. They would arrive inside of the next seven or eight minutes.

Posey lifted the Winchester off the wall and cocked the lever.

The dots became horses and riders as they grew closer. Holding the Winchester, Posey sat with his back against the wall of the roof so they wouldn't see him from a distance.

Pilar appeared on the opposite side of the roof as she came up the ladder.

"What the hell are you doing?" Posey said. "I told you to go into the church."

"I know what you told me," Pilar said. "I decided not to listen."

"Get over here," Posey said.

Pilar raced across the roof, sat next to Posey, and smiled at him.

"Good view," she said.

"Never mind the view and keep your head down," Posey said.

The horses galloped into the village square.

There were a few moments of silence and then a rider said, "Hey, where the hell is everybody?"

Posey turned and looked down at the four riders. He held the Winchester in his arms at the ready.

"United States Marshal," Posey yelled. "I will give you one chance to surrender."

The four riders looked up at him.

Three were hardened-looking men and obvious outlaws. The fourth was a boy, probably not yet eighteen.

"Surrender to who and for what?" one of the men said. "This is Mexico, and your badge ain't worth shit down here."

Posey shot the man in the chest and as he fell off his horse, the other two men reached for their sidearms. Posey cocked the lever of the Winchester and shot both of them. The boy sat on his horse and didn't move except to keep the horse under control.

"Live to be a man or die as a youth. Which will it be, son?" Posey yelled down.

The young rider slowly drew his handgun and tossed it away.

"Step down off that horse and walk to that fountain. Give me your back and don't move until I tell you to," Posey said.

The young rider did as instructed.

"Can you cover him with this rifle?" Posey asked Pilar.

Pilar looked at the Winchester.

"Yes."

Posey gave the Winchester to Pilar and said, "Just aim it in his general direction. If he moves, shoot the ground and he'll stop."

Posey went to the ladder and climbed down. As he came around to the front of the church, two men were still alive on the ground. He pulled the Colt and ended their lives with shots to the chest.

He holstered the Colt and walked to the fountain.

"Turn around, boy," Posey said.

The young rider turned and Posey looked at his face.

"How old are you, boy?" Posey asked.

"Fourteen."

"What the hell are you keeping company with this scum for?" Posey asked.

"No choice."

"What do you mean no choice?"

"My uncle forces me to ride with him."

"Who is your uncle?"

"Pepper Broussard."

"Well, shit," Posey said.

Pilar was suddenly beside Posey. "Do you want me to shoot him?" she said.

"What? No. Give me that," Posey said and snatched the rifle from Pilar.

The church doors opened and the square was suddenly filled with people.

"What's your name?" Posey asked.

"Evan. Evan Broussard."

"Let's go have us a talk," Posey said. "Evan Broussard."

Posey, Evan, and Pilar sat at a table inside

the cantina. Evan ate a huge plate of eggs, beans, and rice with tortillas.

Posey and Pilar had coffee.

"My folks died when I was twelve," Evan said. "My uncle Pepper took me out of school, and I been riding with him since."

"You understand that your uncle is a wanted man, a thief and a murderer?" Posey said. "And will most likely end up on the wrong end of a rope."

"He's the only kin I have left," Evan said.

"He'll put you in the ground before you're eighteen," Posey said. "Is that what you want?"

"No, sir, I don't," Evan said. "But what am I supposed to do? If I run away, my uncle will just find me and beat me or worse. Sometimes I think my uncle is crazy."

Pilar looked at Posey. "You can't put this boy in jail. He is just a child."

Posey took a sip from his cup and set it down. "You have no folks anywhere else?" he asked Evan.

"No, sir. I wish I did," Evan said.

"How did your folks die?" Posey asked.

"My uncle rode in to our house a couple of years ago and wanted to hide from the law," Even said. "My pa said no. My uncle killed him and my ma and then took me with him. Right after that, he hooked up

257

with the outlaw Tom Spooner."

"Your uncle killed your parents?" Pilar asked.

"Yes, ma'am. Shot them both right there in the living room of the house," Evan said. "He set fire to the house before we rode out."

Pilar looked at Posey.

Posey said, "Why did you and the others ride to Nuevo?"

"Tom Spooner wanted to find out what happened to the other four," Evan said.

"Is he planning a job near the border?" Posey said.

"Near as I can figure," Evan said. "I heard him and my uncle talking. They said they could hide out in Nuevo for a few weeks before making their way back to the hideout. By then the law would be looking in the wrong place."

"Do you know what the job is they're planning?" Posey said.

"I didn't hear that part," Evan said. "But I know it's going to be soon."

"How many men do Spooner and your uncle have?" Posey asked.

"Twelve," Evan said. "Well, I guess five now if I do my math right."

"Five plus them. Is that enough to do the job they planned?" Posey asked.

"I don't know."

"Do you know where the hideout is located?" Posey asked.

"Am I going to jail?" Evan said.

"I'll make a deal with you, Evan," Posey said. "You tell me where the hideout is and you won't go to jail. I'll have the US marshals give you a pardon."

Evan stared at Posey for a moment.

"What's a pardon?" Evan asked.

"Forgiveness."

"I guess if you wanted to, you could have just killed me with the others back there," Evan said.

"I could have," Posey said.

"Wyoming," Evan said. "In the Bighorn Mountains."

"Those mountains are a big place, Evan. A man could wander around for years in those mountains. Do you know exactly where the hideout is?"

"I can show you on a map," Evan said.

"I don't have a map," Posey said. "I'll get one when I take you to Laredo."

"Why're you taking me to Laredo?" Evan asked.

"Because you're in Mexico, boy," Posey said.

Evan nodded.

"You stay put," Posey said. "If I have to

chase you, our deal is off. Understand?"

"No problem, Marshal," Evan said. "Can I get some more of these eggs?"

Posey and Pilar met Joseph at the fountain.

"What should we do with the dead men and their horses?" Joseph asked.

"Take their handguns and rifles and lock them in the church for now," Posey said. "Keep any money they have on them, cart them out of town, and have them buried."

"The horses?" Joseph asked.

Posey turned to Pilar. "Can we stash them at your farm for the time being?"

"Yes."

"Joseph, have a few men sit on that kid until I return," he said. "Pilar, can you ride a horse?"

Riding his horse with two horses in tow, Posey looked at Pilar, who rode Evan's horse and towed the fourth.

"Your father did an excellent job this morning," he said.

"My father hates Spooner as much as I do," Pilar said.

They rode to the corral and Pilar dismounted near the cart. She opened the corral gate and Posey led the horses inside and then dismounted. The two mules paid the horses no mind as they grazed on hay.

Jose was on the porch when Pilar and Posey went to the house.

"Four horses means four more dead men?" Joseph asked.

"Three dead men, Papa," Pilar said. "One was just a boy Charlie's age. He is being guarded by Joseph and some others."

"A boy? I don't understand," Jose said.

"It's a long story, Papa," Pilar said.

"I have to get back to town," Posey said.

"Will you come to supper tonight?" Jose asked.

"I think I need to stay close to the village, but thank you," Posey said.

Posey returned to the corral and opened the gate. Pilar followed him and closed the gate when he rode his horse out.

"Do you think more men will come?" Pilar asked.

"I'm not sure," Posey said.

"What about that boy?"

"He'll be fine tonight."

"There is no jail."

"I know."

"He can stay here with us until you decide what to do."

"I'll think about it."

"Then I will ride back with you so he doesn't have to walk."

"I'll bring him," Posey said.

Pilar smiled. "Good, then you can stay for supper."

Riding back to the village Posey felt almost sick to his stomach. When Pilar came up to the roof he had a moment of panic that was similar to that moment of anxiety right before a battle starts.

When he looked at her, he almost felt like he couldn't breathe. Even his hands felt wet and clammy when she was close enough to touch.

Posey wondered if Dale felt that way about Sarah.

Maybe he would ask . . .

He reached the town square of the village and didn't even realize it, he was so lost in thought.

Joseph and some other men were at the mill with Evan.

Posey dismounted at the fountain and walked to the mill.

"I've never seen a mill run by a donkey before," Evan said.

"I expect there are many things you've never seen before," Posey said. "We need to talk."

Evan followed Posey to the fountain where they sat on the wall. Posey rolled a cigarette and lit it with a wood match.

"The job your uncle and Tom Spooner are planning must be close to the border, if they're looking to hide out in Mexico," Posey said.

"I reckon," Even said. "I didn't hear what the job was, but what you said must be so, or why else would they send men to check things out?"

"Where are they hiding out near the border?"

"You mean right now?"

"That's what I mean."

"Camped near the Pecos River maybe ten miles from Del Rio," Evan said.

"That's a two-day ride to Nuevo," Posey said.

"About how long it took us."

Posey smoked and thought for a moment.

"I'm going to wait several days to make sure they don't show up here before I take you to Laredo," Posey said.

"Spooner said to see why the men didn't come back," Evan said. "If nobody goes back, won't he think something's wrong and steer clear?"

"You never know what a man thinks when he's on the run from the law," Posey said. "You think he's going to act one way, and he turns around and does the complete opposite. Understand?"

Evan nodded.

"Tell me about Tom Spooner and your uncle."

"I can't tell you much about Spooner," Evan said. "When he ain't talking with my uncle, he stays to himself mostly. The funny thing is, I seen him do mean things, terrible things, and he never sounds mean or angry. I seen him talk soft and smile while he beat a man to death by pistol whipping."

"And your uncle?"

"My uncle is just plain mean to the bone," Evan said. "He enjoys hurting folks and killing like it was some kind of game."

"I hear he has poor eyesight," Posey said.

"Stand a hundred feet in front of him and he'll put a bullet in your eye slick as can be," Evan said. "Past that, he can't even see a barn right in front of him."

"Why doesn't he get some spectacles?" Posey asked.

"His poor eyes are a sore point with my uncle," Even said. "If you even mention it, he's likely to go crazy and shoot you down."

Posey tossed the spent cigarette. "Do you remember the woman from the cantina? Her name is Pilar."

Evan nodded. "She's a nice lady, and she's pretty."

"Yes, she is," Posey said. "I'm going to bring you to stay with her and her family until I'm ready to take you to Laredo. Is that okay with you?"

"Yes, sir," Evan said.

"Don't get any notions of running away," Posey said. "I'd just track you down and our deal for a pardon would be off."

"No sir, I won't."

"Do you have any gear?"

"On my saddle with my horse."

"Then it's already at the house," Posey said. "I'll give you a ride over on my horse."

"This boy is an outlaw?" Jose said when Posey and Evan walked up to the porch.

"No, Papa, this boy is a boy," Pilar said.

"He's no bigger than me," Charlie said.

"Be quiet, Charlie," Pilar said. "I've heard Billy the Kid was a tiny mouse just like you."

"I'm not an outlaw, sir," Evan said. "My uncle is, and he forces me to ride with him. He killed my parents and took me out of school."

Jose looked at Posey. "The boy can stay here until you need him," he said.

"I appreciate it, Jose," Posey said.

"Robert, Charlie, take Evan inside and show him where he sleeps," Pilar said. "Then set the table for dinner."

■ ■ ■ ■

After supper, Posey, Pilar, and Jose sat in chairs on the porch, each with a mug of coffee. Posey rolled a cigarette.

"Make sure he doesn't wander off," Posey said.

"He will be safe," Jose said.

"I think what might happen is after they pull whatever job they came to Texas to do, Spooner and Broussard will split up their men," Posey said. "I think Spooner and Broussard will ride to their hideout and send the rest of his men here."

"But why, after the others didn't come back?" Pilar asked.

"Neither of them care about their men," Posey said. "They care about money and how to steal it, and they don't care who they have to kill to get it, even their own men. I can't speak for Broussard, but Spooner is as smart as he is crazy. He probably figures the Federales are at the village and killed his men."

"Then why send more?" Pilar asked.

"It makes it harder for the Texas Rangers to follow them if they've split up," Posey said. "I doubt if Spooner or Broussard cares in the least if their men ride into a trap and are killed. It's more loot for them and they can always recruit more men later on down the road when needed."

"I read how Jesse James left his men to die after they robbed that bank in Minnesota," Jose said.

"I see this about the same, except that Spooner knows his men will be riding into an ambush and just doesn't care," Posey said. "Jose, I'm afraid I'm going to ask you to light another signal fire."

"When do you think they will come?" Jose asked.

"Tomorrow, maybe the next day, but soon," Posey said.

"I will be ready," Jose said.

"Pilar, can you ride to the village before dawn tomorrow? I'd like to give you a rifle and a pistol, just in case," Posey said.

"I can ride back with you right now," Pilar said. "I have no problem riding such a short distance in the dark."

"Maybe that would be best," Posey said. "They might be riding at dawn. I'll saddle one of those horses."

"It's been a long day," Posey said as he and Pilar rode to the village square and dismounted at the fountain.

Lights from the cantina spilled out to the

otherwise dark street.

"I told Joseph to hide the guns in the church," Posey said. "Is there some way to lock the door from the outside?"

"It only locks from the inside as far as I know," Pilar said.

"We'll need a light," Posey said. "I'll be right back."

Posey went into the cantina where just a few tables were occupied.

"We are getting ready to close, Marshal," the waitress said in broken English. "Would you like me to hold some food for you?"

"No, but I need to borrow a lantern from a table," Posey said. "And if you could stay open a while, I'd appreciate it."

"Very well, Marshal," the woman said.

Posey took a lantern off a table. "I'll bring this right back."

Pilar was sitting on the church steps and stood up when Posey approached her with the lantern. "Do you know where a closet is?"

"Yes."

Posey handed her the lantern. "Lead the way."

Pilar opened the door to the church and stepped inside and Posey followed.

"Behind the altar," Pilar said.

Her boots echoed loudly on the hardwood

floor as she and Posey walked down the center aisle to the altar.

"The closet behind the altar where the priest used to keep the chalice and wine," Pilar said.

Posey opened the closet door and Pilar brought the lantern closer.

Four Winchester rifles were stacked inside. Four gun belts were wrapped up on the floor. Boxes of ammunition sat on the floor.

Posey selected a rifle and box of ammunition. Then he checked each gun belt and chose a Schofield handgun over the Colt revolvers because the rifle and Schofield used the same ammunition.

"Let's get these on the horse," Posey said as he closed the closet door.

They returned to the horses, and Posey put the Winchester in the saddle sleeve and the ammunition in the saddlebags. He hung the Schofield by the holster over the saddle horn.

"The moon will be up soon," Posey said. "I think you should wait until it's light enough to see riding back."

"I can find my way home with my eyes closed," Pilar said. "But I will do as you ask."

"I asked the cantina to stay open for me

so we can wait for the moon to rise," Posey said.

Pilar and Posey entered the cantina. All tables were empty now. Pilar set the lantern on a table as the woman came from out back.

"Pilar, what are you doing out so late?" she asked.

"She's bringing something to her father for me," Posey said. "I'd like to wait for the moon to rise, if that's all right with you."

"Of course. It won't be long and I have some coffee left," the woman said.

"We could use a cup," Pilar said.

The woman went to the kitchen.

Posey pulled out his pouch and papers and rolled a cigarette. By the time he lit it with a wood match, the woman returned with two mugs of coffee.

"Thank you," Posey said.

"I will be in the kitchen," the woman said.

Posey took a sip of the hot, sweet coffee and looked at Pilar.

"Do you ever think about other things besides your work?" she asked.

"I don't . . . I'm not sure I know what you mean," Posey said.

"Do you have a woman back home?" Pilar asked.

"Actually, I don't," Posey said.

"Why not?"

"I guess it's a question of time," Posey said. "There never seems to be enough of it to do the things a man wants."

"I see," Pilar said. "And what is it that you want?"

Posey thought for a moment. "To go home," he said.

"Where is home?"

"A little farm in Missouri near the Arkansas border," Posey said. "Three hundred acres of prime bottomland that will grow anything. Good land for horses, too."

"You are a farmer?" Pilar said, somewhat shocked.

"Used to be a long time ago," Posey said. "Before the war."

"I want to know more," Pilar said.

The woman came from the kitchen. "The moon is up, Pilar," she said.

"We best get you home," Posey said.

Pilar stared at Posey for a moment. "Yes," she finally said.

Posey walked her to the horses and he stood at the fountain and watched her ride away to her farm, her silhouette atop the horse fading into the distance in the soft moonlight.

CHAPTER TWENTY-SEVEN

Posey climbed up to the rooftop of the church shortly before dawn. He brought the Winchester and Sharps rifles with him. The Sharps was fed one round at a time, and he loaded his shirt pocket with ammunition for the massive weapon.

As the sun rose, Posey felt weary and tired. Sleep escaped him last night. It seemed every time he drifted off, Pilar invaded his thoughts and woke him up. Her silhouette in the moonlight was enough to weaken his knees. He'd push the image from his mind, and it would just return again.

There wasn't time for women; he didn't have the right anyway, and he knew that. He'd made a promise to Dale and he planned to keep it, no matter what.

But the promise was flawed.

He wasn't tracking Tom Spooner to bring him to justice because he believed in the law or because it was right, but because he wanted revenge against the man who sent him to prison.

And money.

There it was for all to see.

Revenge and money.

The backbone of all evil.

"*Señor* Marshal, I have brought you some breakfast," the woman from the cantina said.

Posey turned around as she set a tray on the church rooftop.

"Thank you, ma'am," he said.

"I will be back later for the tray," she said.

"Maybe when you come back, you could bring more coffee?"

She smiled and nodded and disappeared as she climbed down the ladder.

Posey ate, watching the horizon. He couldn't see from here, but somehow he knew Pilar would be in the cart with her father.

He lied to her, of course, when he wrapped her in his blanket and placed her on his saddle. He did look, and the sight of her body had haunted him since. He saw her in his dreams and in his thoughts.

"You haven't the right," he said aloud.

"You should not be here," Jose said.

Pilar and Jose sat in the cart with the rifle between them on the seat. Around Pilar's waist was the Schofield pistol. They spoke in Spanish.

"If something happens, Papa, what then?" Pilar said. "With your poor eyesight, you'd probably shoot yourself in the foot."

"There is nothing wrong with my eyesight," Jose said.

"You are blind as a Mexican fruit bat, Papa," Pilar said.

Jose sighed. "Only at short distances. Give a man some coffee then," he said.

Pilar turned, reached into the cart for the metal pail, and removed the cover. There were two cups and she filled both, then replaced the cover. She gave one cup to Jose.

Jose took a sip of coffee. "The marshal is a handsome man," he said.

"I haven't noticed," Pilar said.

"Really?" Jose said, as he smiled and took another sip. "Such dark circles under your eyes. Did you not sleep well last night after your ride with him to town?"

"Drink your coffee, Papa, and be quiet," Pilar said.

Last night was the longest, most lonely night of her life. When she left Posey at the fountain, she wanted to jump off the horse and run to his arms. She wanted to go to his room and lie with him in bed. Instead she cried the entire way home, glad for the cover of darkness.

That was a sin, such thoughts, but the priest was dead and there was no one to hear her confession, so what did it matter if she had such thoughts.

"As soon as his job is finished, he will go home," Jose said.

"I know that, Papa."

"And when he goes home, you will never see him again," Jose said. "What then?"

Pilar looked at Jose.

"I wish your mother was here," Jose said. "She would know how to talk with you on such matters. She died far too soon."

Pilar sighed at the mention of her mother. Her mother would never approve of her behavior and would do everything in her power to ensure that Pilar married a Mexican farmer as she'd done.

"Papa, have you ever wished for more?" she asked.

"More what?"

"Just more."

"I have land, three healthy children, and the love of a woman I loved more than anything," Jose said. "What more can a man ask for out of life?"

Pilar sipped her coffee.

"Maybe some lunch?" she said.

"Yes, that would be good," Jose agreed.

Posey used his bandanna to wipe sweat from his face and eyes. The Mexican sun was blistering hot on his back, and his shirt was soaked through.

He asked Joseph to bring him a bucket of water and a ladle, and he used the ladle to pour water over his head. He didn't bother to wipe it away but let it evaporate.

Down below, the mill was in use. Farmers were grinding corn and wheat by the cartful. Joseph and others were engaged in conversation and Posey's Spanish wasn't good, but he could guess what the topic was.

Posey stood and stretched his back.

The sky was bright blue, without a cloud in sight.

Jose and Pilar had just finished eating the stew she had made for lunch when five riders thundered past the cornfield.

Pilar stood up and Jose said, "Wait," and took out his pocket watch.

The riders were traveling twice as fast as the first group so he would cut the time in half to start the fire.

"Go wait by the hay and start the fire when I tell you to," Jose said.

Pilar jumped down and went to the round pile of stones. She took a wood match from her shirt pocket and looked at Jose.

He was looking at his pocket watch. Finally, he looked at her, nodded, and Pilar struck the match against a stone.

The clouds of white smoke rising from the cornfield caught Posey's eye immediately.

"Joseph, the church. Hurry," he shouted down to Joseph.

Within a minute, the square was empty.

Posey watched the riders coming hard. There were five of them. He didn't need to see their faces to know Spooner and Broussard weren't among them. They were fifteen hundred yards away and riding fast.

Posey picked up the Sharps rifle and aimed it at the riders so he could adjust the rear sights. Then he removed a cartridge from his shirt pocket and loaded the massive weapon.

He removed four additional cartridges from the pocket and lined them up on the wall to his left.

Posey knew from years of experience as a soldier and sniper how to judge distances. He waited until the riders were approximately five hundred yards away and then took careful aim at the center rider.

He took a shallow breath, held it, and squeezed the trigger.

About one and a half seconds after the booming noise of the shot, the center rider fell from his horse.

Before the remaining four riders even realized what had happened, Posey reloaded and fired a second round, taking out the rider on the far right.

The remaining three riders slowed to a stop and didn't move.

Until the rider on the far left fell from his horse from Posey's third shot.

The remaining two riders turned their horses and raced east.

Posey could have killed them both, but there was no need. They wouldn't come to the village and would cross the border back to Texas, where they would be caught or killed by the rangers.

Posey lowered the Sharps and watched them ride away.

After setting the hay on fire, Pilar ran to the end of the field and watched the riders gallop toward the village.

The riders appeared as black dots on the horizon.

Suddenly, the dot in the middle fell from his horse. Two seconds later, she heard the crack of a rifle. Then another dot fell, followed by another shot, and after that, one more rider fell, followed by a third rifle crack.

The remaining two dots turned east and raced away.

No more shots fired. Posey let them live because there was no reason to kill them, just like with the boy, Evan.

She returned to the cart.

"It's over, Papa," she said.

"Let's go back to the house and wait for your marshal," Jose said.

"He isn't my marshal, Papa," Pilar said.

"If you say so," Jose said.

Posey arrived with the horses of the three men he shot in tow. He dismounted at the corral and walked to the porch where Pilar sat, waiting.

"I saw the men fall from their horses," Pilar said. "You could have killed the other two but didn't."

"No need. They got the message."

Jose came out from the house and looked at Posey.

"My sons and the boy, Evan, are in the north field watering the crops," Jose said. "I don't expect them back until dark. He is a good boy, this Evan."

"I'll be picking him up in the morning to take him to Laredo," Posey said.

Jose looked at the corral. "What about these horses?"

"Not counting Evan's, there are ten horses for you to divide up among the village as you see fit," Posey said. "At least you get something for your troubles."

"Will you come back for supper?" Pilar asked.

"Reckon not," Posey said. "There are bodies to be buried and such."

"I see," Pilar said with sadness in her voice. "Then we will say goodbye in the morning."

"Reckon so," Posey said.

He left the porch and returned to his horse. "I'll be back after breakfast for the boy," Posey said.

Shirtless, drenched in sweat, Posey tossed the last shovelful of dirt on the final grave.

Standing beside him, shovel in hand, Joseph said, "We are running out of places to stick dead outlaws."

Posey grinned. "Did you take what money they had and their weapons?"

"Yes."

"Divide it any way you see fit."

"Your job is done then?"

"Yes."

"You will leave then?"

"Yes, but right now I want a shave, a hot bath, and a good meal," Posey said.

The atmosphere in the cantina was almost carnival-like. Every table was occupied, and someone even played the guitar.

Weary, Posey went to his tiny room behind the cantina and stripped off his shirt, gun belt, and boots and flopped onto the bed.

He closed his eyes and didn't open them again until something outside his door woke him up.

CHAPTER TWENTY-EIGHT

Posey's eyes snapped open at the sound of a footstep outside his door. Moonlight filtered in through the open window and he looked at his gun belt on the table beside the bed and reached for the Colt.

Holding the Colt, he sat up in bed and quietly cocked the hammer. Barefoot, he slowly stood up and silently walked to the door.

He stood still and listened. A shadow cast under the door. Someone was standing right outside, waiting.

Posey's first thought was an assassin sent by Spooner.

The door had no lock, and whoever was on the other side could have easily shoved it open and shot him before he got out of bed, but they hadn't.

Holding the Colt at the ready, Posey yanked open the door and looked at Pilar. Dressed in pants, a dark shirt, and her Stetson hat, in the moonlight she appeared breathtaking.

"Jesus Christ, woman, I could have shot you," he said as he uncocked the Colt.

"But you didn't," Pilar said.

"What are you doing here?" Posey asked. "It's the middle of the night."

Pilar walked into the room, turned, and looked at Posey.

"You are either too shy or too stupid or maybe both to seduce a woman, so I am here to do it for you," she said.

One candle on the small table beside the bed provided just enough light to see. Posey looked at Pilar's naked body, and he felt weak and disoriented.

"I am not sorry about this," Pilar said. "Are you?"

"Yes," Posey said.

"Why?"

"Because I'm not who you think I am," Posey said.

Pilar sat up in the bed. "Tell me who you are," she said.

Posey sighed. "Not two months ago, I was in Yuma Prison. Do you know what Yuma Prison is?"

"Yes. In Arizona."

"Then you know I am not a good man,"

Posey said.

"I'll judge that for myself," Pilar said. "Start from the beginning and tell me why you were in prison."

About an hour later, Posey rolled a cigarette and lit it from the candle's flame and said, "That's everything there is to know about me."

"You are not an outlaw," Pilar said. "Your brother would not have trusted you with that badge if you were. An outlaw would not have stayed and helped our village or that boy, Evan. I don't believe you want to find Tom Spooner for revenge or money, but because you made a promise to your brother. And I will tell you something else, Jack Posey. You love me. I can see it in your eyes and in the way I make you so nervous. Don't deny it, and you might as well say it."

Posey looked at Pilar.

"It's okay to say the words," Pilar said. "If you say them, your manhood won't fall off. I promise."

"Yes, I do love you," Posey said. "But I don't know what it amounts to."

"It amounts to a lot," Pilar said.

Posey put the cigarette out and placed his head on the pillow next to Pilar.

"Where did you learn English so well?" he asked.

"I was born in Texas," Pilar said. "My father moved us to Mexico when the war broke out to escape the destruction."

"So you're an American?" Posey said.

"As is my father," Pilar said. "He was born in Texas. My mother died in childbirth with Charlie."

"I'm sorry."

"Me too."

"I have to finish this," Posey said.

"I know."

"Would you . . . what I mean is . . . I'd like to come back," Posey said.

"You idiot. I want you to come back," Pilar said.

"To bring you to Missouri, to my farm," Posey said.

"On one condition," Pilar said. "That when you come back for me, you have a ring in your pocket or I won't go."

"I can do that," Posey said.

"It will be light soon," Pilar said. "I have to get back before my father wakes up."

"I know."

Pilar rolled over on top of Posey and kissed him. "We have a little time," she said.

Posey ate breakfast alone in the cantina. Afterward, Joseph and other villagers said goodbye to him as he saddled his horse at the fountain.

"We hope you come back someday, Marshal," Joseph said.

"I have to, Joseph," Posey said as he mounted the saddle. "There's no place in America a man can get a shot of tequila."

Posey rode to Pilar's house, lost in thought. A man can lie to the world, but not to himself. He did love Pilar, right down to his bones.

He hoped, in his heart, that he was good enough for her.

Joseph, Robert, Charlie, and Evan were on the porch when Posey arrived at the house.

Evan's horse was saddled at the corral.

Posey dismounted and walked to the porch and looked at Evan. "Are you ready, son?" he asked.

"Yes, Marshal."

Posey looked at Jose. "Where is Pilar? I'd like to say goodbye."

"She went to the north field early this morning."

"Why?"

"Go ask her," Jose said.

Posey went to his horse, mounted the saddle, and rode north about three hundred yards to a large field of wheat.

"Pilar, where are you?" he shouted as he

dismounted, but she didn't respond.

He could see the impressions of her boots where she entered the field and he followed them about a hundred feet and found her sitting in the dirt.

"What are you doing?" Posey asked.

"Crying."

"Why?" Posey said as he lifted Pilar to her feet.

"You better keep that promise to me, Jack Posey," Pilar said.

"The only thing that could stop me is if I'm dead," Posey said.

"That's why I'm crying, you fool," Pilar said.

"Come on, I'll ride you back to the house," Posey said.

"Can we walk back? I don't want my father to see me crying."

"I think your father is a much smarter man than you give him credit for," Posey said.

"How long will it take us to reach Laredo?" Evan asked.

"Late afternoon, I'm guessing," Posey said.

They were riding north toward the Rio Grande River where Posey had crossed when riding south.

"I thought you said we need to go to Santa Fe," Evan said.

"We do, but it would be a lot quicker if we took the railroad," Posey said.

"I've never been on the railroad," Evan said.

"We'll make it to Santa Fe in ten or twelve hours," Posey said. "Instead of weeks and weeks in the saddle."

"The railroad moves that fast?"

"Faster than the fastest horse," Posey said. "Maybe fifty miles an hour or more."

"I don't know what that means," Evan said.

"It means we'll get to Santa Fe a hell of a lot quicker, that's what it means," Posey said.

"Where do we get the railroad?"

"Houston."

"Houston, the city?"

"Since Sam Houston died nearly twenty years ago, I reckon it's the city."

"I never been to a city."

"Been to a town?"

"A few."

"Same thing, only bigger."

"When I was in school, I read about places like Boston and New York and a place called Paris, France, in Europe," Evan said. "Europe is a place on the other side of the ocean. I never thought I'd see a real city."

"You live long enough and you see everything worth seeing," Posey said.

"Can I ask you something?"

"Go ahead."

"Why didn't you kill those last two men?"

"A man doesn't kill another man when he's running away," Posey said. "That's something a coward would do."

"My uncle would have killed them," Evan said.

"I expect he would have," Posey said. "We're coming to the river."

Posey followed the river to the spot where he had crossed before and dismounted. "The silt is high. Should be an easy crossing, but keep your horse behind mine."

Posey took his horse into the water and Evan followed. With the water level low and the silt high, it took only minutes to cross.

"Let's give the horses a break," Posey said. "Gather some wood and I'll make us some coffee."

Posey and Evan ate strips of jerky and drank coffee while the horses rested and grazed on grass.

"Pilar is a pretty woman," Evan said.

"Yes, she is," Posey said as he bit off a hunk of jerky.

"And kind."

"I agree."

"I think she's sweet on you," Evan said. "I saw her crying when we left. Girls don't cry for no reason unless they're hurt or sad. I think she was sad you was leaving."

"Know what I think?" Posey asked. "I think we need to push on if we're to make Laredo before dark."

They reached Laredo by late afternoon. The sprawling town was filled with cowboys off the trail, soldiers and townsfolk. Evan looked around in wonder as they rode through the crowded streets.

"At the end of this street is the Texas Rangers office. We'll stop there," Posey said.

They rode to the office, dismounted, and tied the horses to the hitching post.

Posey opened the office door and stepped inside, followed by Evan.

Captain McDonald and Scout were the only two rangers inside the office. McDonald sat behind a desk.

"I'll be damned," McDonald said.

"I just stopped by for a steak," Posey said. "Care to join me?"

At the Laredo Hotel, Posey, Scout, McDonald, and Evan found a table in the dining room and ordered steaks.

Posey gave McDonald a brief report on his stay in Nuevo.

"Damnedest thing," McDonald said. "Spooner robbed the Overland Stage carrying the payroll to the railroad construction at Eagle Pass. They split up and some headed to Mexico, but we didn't know if Spooner was with them. By the time we reached Eagle Pass, we lost the trail of the other two."

"This boy is Evan Broussard," Posey said. "His uncle is Pepper Broussard."

"I'll be damned," McDonald said.

"He helped me down in Nuevo," Posey said. "He might know where Spooner and Pepper are hiding out. We need some good maps of the Bighorn Mountains."

"All we got are maps of Texas," McDonald said.

"I figured," Posey said. "I'm taking him to Santa Fe to get a pardon. I'll find some maps there. Right now, me and the boy are checking into the hotel and having us a bath."

"A bath?" Evan said.

"Son, downwind of you makes a man's eyes water," Posey said.

"Don't be afraid of that soap, boy," Posey

said. "And use it good on your hair. You got enough grease in your hair to make lantern oil out of."

"I don't see what good it does to get all cleaned up just to put on the same dirty clothes," Evan said.

"Good point," Posey said. "When we get back to the room, I'll go to the store and pick you up some new clothes."

"I got no money," Evan said.

"You can owe me," Posey said.

Evan scrubbed his hair with the soap. "What's gonna happen to me?" he asked. "I got no kin to live with. Will they send me to one of them homes?"

"Not if I can help it," Posey said.

Evan dunked under to rinse his hair, popped up, and said, "Do you like being a marshal?"

"If I had a choice, I'd rather be working the fields of my farm," Posey said.

"You're a farmer?" Evan said with shock.

"I was once," Posey said. "I'd like to be again. Come on, we're clean enough."

Walking along the wood sidewalk with a wrapped bundle under his arm, Posey spotted McDonald sitting in a chair in front of the hotel.

"Thought I'd save you and the boy some

trouble," McDonald said. "I wired the railroad in Houston. They'll have a special car waiting for you at the construction site to take you to Houston tomorrow whenever you can get there. The site is about a full day's ride northeast."

"I'm obliged to you, Captain," Posey said.

"You killed most of Spooner's gang. It's the least I can do," McDonald said.

"We'll get an early start then," Posey said. "If you're up, join us for breakfast."

Posey tossed the package on one of two beds in the hotel room. "Two shirts, two pairs of pants, the like amount in socks and underwear, and one nightshirt to sleep in," he said.

"I never had new clothes all at once," Evan said. "Sometimes a shirt or pants, but never at the same time."

"Put on the nightshirt and get to bed," Posey said. "We got an early start in the morning."

"Yes, sir," Evan said.

Posey was close to sleep when he heard the boy roll over in his bed.

"Marshal," Evan whispered. "Are you awake?"

"I am now," Posey said. "What is it?"

"My uncle would shoot you in the back,"

Evan said. "He'd shoot a blind man and not think twice about it."

"I'll keep that in mind," Posey said and closed his eyes.

Pilar came to him in his dreams. Her body was warm to the touch. Her hair was soft and smooth, and he buried his face in it and took in the scent of her soap.

They were making love in the little room behind the cantina when there was a noise and he reached for his Colt.

Posey opened his eyes.

Whatever happens, don't let Pepper Broussard shoot you in the back, he thought.

CHAPTER TWENTY-NINE

When Posey and Evan stepped out to the front porch of the hotel, they found McDonald and Scout waiting for them in chairs.

"You're up early," Posey said. "It's still dark."

"Wanted to make sure we saw you before you left," McDonald said. "Scout has volunteered to accompany you."

"I appreciate it, Scout, but I think I can find the railroad construction site okay," Posey said.

McDonald shook his head. "All the way to the Bighorn Mountains," he said.

"I didn't think the rangers ever left Texas," Posey said.

"Scout is actually an army scout assigned to me," McDonald said. "No better tracker anywhere. We figure we owe you for taking out most of Spooner's gang. If anybody can make it through the Bighorns, it's Scout here."

"I figure he'd be gone a month or more," Posey said.

"I can do a month standing on my head, and besides, my wife will be glad to be rid of me for a while," Scout said.

"I need to get Evan to Santa Fe before we head out," Posey said.

"We'll leave right after we have some breakfast," Scout said.

"By the way, I never did thank you for the watch," Posey said.

"Small price for ten dead outlaws," Mc-Donald said.

Scout kept them moving at a fast pace for several hours. Posey's horse had no trouble keeping up, but Evan's smaller horse lagged behind a bit.

Around noon, Scout called for a break.

"We'll rest the horses for one hour," Scout said. "We'll likely be early and have to wait for the train."

Posey leaned against a tree and rolled a cigarette.

"Are you in the army?" Evan asked Scout.

"I scout for the army, but I ain't in it," Scout said. "That's how I came to scout for the rangers. They sort of made a loan of me where needed. I kinda found a home with the rangers, but the army still pays me."

"Could I join the army?" Evan asked.

"Don't see why not, when you is old enough."

"Even though my uncle is an outlaw?"

"What your uncle does has got nothing to do with what you do," Scout said. "Each man gets judged on his own actions."

"What about being a marshal or Texas Ranger?" Evan asked.

"A man can be whatever he wants to, good or bad," Scout said. "It's his choice. But first you got to grow up. When you do, you'll make the right choice for what suits you best."

"What's your real name, Scout?" Evan asked.

"Sebastian O'Leary," Scout said. "But no one calls me anything but Scout, even my wife and five kids. Now we best get moving."

Evan looked at the hundred or so men laying track at the construction site, having never seen so many men working in one place before.

"Down the track a ways is where we catch the train," Scout said.

A thousand yards from where the men were working, Scout, Posey, and Evan dismounted.

"Keep your eye on the tracks coming from the east down yonder," Scout told Evan. "You'll see the train long before it gets here."

"How?" Evan said.

"You'll see," Scout said.

While Evan watched the tracks in the distance, Posey rolled a cigarette and lit it with a wood match.

Scout came and stood beside Posey.

"He's a good boy," Scout said. "What's going to happen to him?"

"My brother in Santa Fe is a territorial marshal," Posey said. "He'll see the boy is pardoned of any crimes he may have been forced to commit by his uncle."

"And then?"

"I don't know."

"If the boy is agreeable, when we done with this, he could come back with me," Scout said. "My oldest boy is about his age, and he'll earn his keep and go to school."

"Ask the boy," Posey said.

"Hey, Marshal, Mister Scout, I see clouds of black smoke," Evan said.

"That would be the iron horse coming to take us to Houston," Scout said.

It took about ten minutes for the three-car train to arrive, and when it slowly rolled past them, Evan was bewitched at the sight of the massive locomotive, riding car, and boxcar.

When the train finally halted, Posey said, "Evan, let's get the horses loaded into the boxcar. Slide open the door and pull down the ramp."

The engineer left the car and walked to Posey. "Are you Marshal Posey?"

"I am," Posey said.

The engineer nodded. "Let's go to Houston," he said.

Evan stared out the window and watched the countryside whiz by at fifty miles an hour, so fast it all appeared to him as a blur.

"We'll make Houston by seven o'clock tonight," Scout said. "After they take on water and coal, we'll head out directly to Santa Fe."

"Just us?" Evan asked.

"The railroad owes the rangers a great deal," Scout said. "We fought Indians, robbers, and everything in between for them, so paying us back a favor don't bother them none."

"How far is Santa Fe from Houston?" Evan asked.

"About nine hundred miles," Scout said.

"We'll make the trip in about fifteen hours or so."

"Nine hundred miles," Evan said with wonderment as he looked out the window.

Grinning, Posey lowered his hat over his eyes and took a nap.

"This is Houston," Posey said as they exited the train at a rear platform.

It wasn't yet dark, and Evan stared at the massive city in front of him. "I didn't know a town could be so big," he said.

The engineer approached Posey.

"You have time to grab some supper," he said. "But I'd like to leave around eight-thirty."

Scout and Posey watched Evan eat a second helping of apple pie at a restaurant a few blocks from the railroad station.

"I never ate at a real restaurant before except for that little place in Mexico with you, Marshal," Evan said.

"Then this is your first," Posey said. "Now, if you don't want a third slice, I suggest we walk the horses for a bit before we leave to stretch their legs."

Fifteen hours later, around one-thirty in the afternoon, the three-car train pulled into the Santa Fe railroad depot.

"Let's get the horses and walk to my brother's house," Posey said.

At the boxcar, Posey shook the engineer's hand. "Appreciate the help," he said.

"Return the favor and catch that son of a bitch," the engineer said.

"It's a good stretch of the legs to my brother's house," Posey told Evan. "The horses can use it."

As they walked the horses from the railroad station to the Posey home, Scout said, "Me and the boy discussed it while you was taking a nap, and he's agreeable to coming back to Texas with me if that's all right with the law."

"Ask my brother, but I don't see why not," Posey said.

When they reached Dale's home, the screen door opened and Sarah came out and stood on the porch. She didn't need to say a word; her face said it all.

Trouble.

"He took Erin," Sarah said. "Tom Spooner took Erin."

Posey rushed up to the porch and she grabbed him, put her head on his shoulder, and burst into tears.

In the parlor, Posey smoked a cigarette and

said, "Tell me what happened from the beginning."

Posey and Sarah were on the love seat.

Scout and Evan stood quietly in the corner of the room.

"Two . . . nights ago . . . it was the middle of the night," Sarah said. "I don't know how they got into the house. There —"

"How many men?" Posey asked.

"Two. One was Tom Spooner," Sarah said. "That's what Dale called him. The other man, Dale said was an outlaw called Pepper Broussard."

Posey nodded. "Back up and tell me what happened."

"Dale heard a noise in the house," Sarah said. "He got his gun and went to see what it was. He lit the lantern in the living room and went to check the bedrooms when there was a scream. Erin was screaming in her room. I got out of bed and Dale was in Erin's bedroom. He was saying something like, 'Please don't hurt her,' or something like that. I stood behind Dale and the man with the scar had a gun to Erin's head."

Posey said, "And then?"

"The other one, Spooner, he came up behind me and put his hand over my mouth," Sarah said. "He tied me and John to a chair and put gags over our mouths so we couldn't scream."

"Sarah, where's Dale?" Posey asked.

"At the doctor's office."

"Why?"

"They tied Dale's hands behind his back to a chair where I could see him," Sarah said. "And gagged his mouth. The man with the scar, he said he wanted to kill us all, but Spooner said he had something else in mind. Dale was in a nightshirt and Spooner saw the wound in his leg. Dale was still limping, but it had healed nicely. He took his knife and stabbed Dale right in the wound, right down to the bone. Then Spooner said if we want to see Erin again, we were to tell you he'll been waiting for you and to come alone. He said if he saw anyone else besides you, he'd kill Erin on the spot."

"Spooner said that? He'd be waiting for me?" Posey asked. "Did he say where?"

"No."

Posey put the cigarette out in the glass ashtray on the table in front of the love seat and then stood up.

"This is Scout," Posey said. "At least that's what they call him in Texas. The boy is Evan Broussard, Pepper Broussard's nephew, but don't hold it against him. He's a good boy and he's helped me. Watch him until I get back."

"I'll go with you," Scout said.

"Jack, he could lose the leg," Sarah said.

Dale was in a back room on the second floor of Doctor Baker's office. He was conscious, but heavily sedated on morphine when Posey and Scout arrived.

"He lost a great deal of blood and he's very weak," Baker said. "And infection has set in on the bone. He sat in that chair until morning when his deputies came to the house. About six hours in that chair, bleeding from an open wound, it became septic."

"Could he lose the leg?" Posey asked.

"There is that possibility."

"Can you do anything to save it?"

"I'm doing all I can for him here," Baker said. "As soon as he's stable, I'm sending him to the big hospital in Minnesota."

"Can I see him?"

"Just for a minute. I'll take you to him."

Baker led Posey to a back bedroom, one of four. Dale was on his back, propped up with pillows in the bed.

"I keep his head high so his lungs stay clear," Baker said.

"Is he awake?" Posey said.

"Yes, but in sort of a fog."

Posey stood over the bed. "Dale?" he

whispered. "It's Jack."

Slowly Dale opened his eyes. They were glazed over as he focused on Posey.

"Jack?" Dale said.

"I'm here, brother," Posey said.

"They took my little girl, Jack," Dale said. "They took Erin."

"I know," Posey said. "I'm going after them. Dale, it's important for you to tell me what Spooner said as best you can remember."

"He said if we wanted to see Erin alive again, I was to tell you he'd be waiting for you," Dale said. "And to come alone."

"Where, Dale? Did he say where?"

"I asked him that," Dale said. "He said you'd know. Then he put a gag in my mouth, shoved a knife into my leg, and left. What did he mean, you'd know? How would you know, Jack? How?"

"I got a lead on him, Dale," Posey said.

"A lead? Where have you been all this time?"

"On his trail. Texas, Mexico, and I'll find her, Dale. Don't you worry about that. I'll find her."

Dale reached for Jack and tried to sit up. "She's just eight years old, Jack," he said.

"That's enough," Baker said. "Marshal, you lie down now and rest."

"Don't worry, Dale," Posey said. "I'll get her back."

Posey left the bedroom and found Scout outside the doctor's office.

"Let's get Evan," Posey said.

At the kitchen table, Sarah poured coffee for Posey and Scout.

"Where's the boy?" Posey asked.

"With John in his room," Sarah said and took a seat at the table.

"We're going after Erin first thing in the morning," Posey said.

Sarah looked at Scout. "You and . . . ?"

"Call me Scout, ma'am," Scout said.

"Just the two of you?" Sarah asked.

"Spooner is crazy, but not stupid," Posey said. "He'll know if more than one or two came after him, and we'll never get Erin back."

"I'm going with you," Sarah said.

"Impossible," Posey said.

"She's my daughter," Sarah said.

"When was the last time you rode a horse?" Posey asked.

Sarah looked down at the table and didn't answer.

"Your place is with Dale," Posey said.

"No disrespect intended, ma'am, but where we going is no place for a lady," Scout said. "I've been tracking for near twenty-five years, and I give you my word we'll find your little girl."

Sarah stared at Posey and Scout, and then she burst into tears.

"Where are we going?" Evan asked as he, Posey, and Scout walked along the wood sidewalks of Santa Fe.

"Here," Posey said as they reached the federal marshal's office.

Posey opened the door. Two of Dale's deputies were seated at desks.

"We need maps of Wyoming Territory," Posey said. "Any and all."

Posey studied the maps spread out on Dale's desk.

"Show me," he said.

Evan put a finger on the map. "I been there three times, and I got a real good memory," he said. "We rode to here, this little town called Buffalo about a day's ride from the pass in the mountains."

"South, east, north from Buffalo?" Posey asked.

"East mostly and maybe a bit to the north," Evan said. "I think my uncle called it Johnson County."

Posey and Scout studied the maps.

"Where do you enter the mountains?" Posey asked.

"My uncle called it the red wall," Evan said. "About here on the map I figure."

Evan touched a spot on the Bighorn Mountains.

"Red wall?" Posey said.

"Red sandstone," Scout said. "I seen it before."

"Then what?" Posey asked.

"Maybe halfway along the red wall is a V-shaped canyon that narrows to like a funnel shape," Evan said. "You follow the funnel maybe a day and a half and you come to this hidden valley. That's where they hide out. They got a cabin there and everything."

"Cabin?" Scout said.

"Yes, sir, a right big cabin," Evan said. "I slept in one of them. Last year my uncle and Spooner rustled a hundred head of cattle off a ranch in Casper. Spooner laughed that the rancher never even knew it."

Posey looked at Scout. "Do you think you can find it?"

Scout nodded. "I can find it," he said.

Posey looked at the map. "The railroad can take us to Cheyenne. We'll ride the rest of the way north to Buffalo and start from there."

"I can take you," Evan said. "I know the way."

"Can't allow that, son," Posey said. "Maybe if you were eighteen or close to it, but you're too young."

"But I've been there," Evan said.

"Listen to the marshal, Evan," Scout said. "I'm depending on you to come back to Texas with me. I can't put you in danger like this before you have the chance to grow up. I'll find the pass."

"Take those maps back to the house," Posey said. "I'm going to see my brother."

"All I wanted was revenge on Tom Spooner for setting me up for a prison stretch," Posey said. "And then to return to the farm to dig up the money I buried there back in 'seventy-seven and disappear. Maybe go north to Montana or south into Mexico. I lied to you to get the pardon, and I had no intentions of keeping my end once I killed Tom Spooner."

"What money, Jack?"

"After the war, all those places me and Tom raided to get even for what they did to our parents. I never spent a penny of it, Dale. When me and Spooner split up, I didn't take a nickel of all the money we robbed that had nothing to do with losing the farm. I let Spooner keep it all. I buried the money in a strongbox along the south wall we dug up one summer to make a new field. Remember?"

"I remember."

"Right under the giant tree we built the wall around rather than cut it down and dig up the stump," Posey said.

"I know the tree," Dale said. "How much did you bury?"

"Twenty-two thousand in gold coins."

"Jeeze."

"I figured after I killed Tom, I'd be on my merry way with my pockets full of gold," Posey said. "But something happened."

Dale sat up a bit against the pillows. "What happened?" he asked. "What happened, Jack?"

"I . . . it's the respect people pay to the badge you pinned on me, Dale," Posey said. "I can't explain it, but people look at you different when you wear one of these."

Posey tapped the badge on his shirt.

"In Texas, the rangers helped me find where Spooner sometimes hides," Posey said. "A little town called Nuevo across the Rio Grande in Mexico. Spooner hides there sometimes and terrorizes the farmers who live there. I killed about ten of Spooner's men. That's why he came for Erin. He figured if he had Erin, I'd come after him, and he figured right."

"You killed ten of his men?" Dale asked.

"I spared a few, plus a boy. Broussard's nephew. He's just a kid, but he knows where Spooner's hideout is in the Bighorns," Posey said. "I told the boy you would get him a pardon for riding with his uncle, even though he had no choice after Broussard murdered his parents."

"Murdered his parents? How old is the boy?"

"Fourteen."

"Aw, hell, Jack, he doesn't need a pardon, he needs a set of parents," Dale said.

"A Texan, a scout for the army, is going to take him back to Texas to live with his wife and five kids," Posey said.

"Got it all figured out, Jack."

"Not all," Posey said. "That money I buried."

"It doesn't belong to anybody anymore, Jack," Dale said. "I wouldn't know who to return it to, so you might as well keep it."

"I figured," Posey said. "I want you to do something for me if I don't make it back. Dig up the money and take it down to Nuevo and give it to a woman named Pilar Lobos. Her family has a small farm right outside of town."

"Why?" Dale asked.

"Because I'm asking you to."

"No, stupid, why this woman?" Dale said. "Who is she?"

"If I make it back, she's going to be my wife."

"The hell you say."

"Will you do that for me if I don't make it back?"

"All right, Jack."

"We leave in the morning for the Bighorns," Posey said. "And I swear I'll be back with Erin."

"Jack, you can wear that badge permanently," Dale said.

Posey grinned. "The hell you say."

Dale sighed. "On the way out, Jack, tell the doctor I could use some morphine."

After supper, Posey, Scout, and Sarah sat in chairs on the porch. Posey and Scout had cups of coffee.

Posey rolled a cigarette.

"We'll be leaving first thing tomorrow," Posey said.

"Tomorrow is Sunday," Sarah said. "The railroad doesn't run until noon. Most of the town will be at services to pray for Erin. I expect you and Mr. Scout to attend as well."

"Yes, ma'am," Scout said.

"Jack, my daughter can't die at the age of eight," Sarah said. "Without knowing what it's like to have a boy kiss her for the first time. To fall in love and marry and have children and a home of her own. To grow old with the man she loves and someday have grandchildren. She can't be cheated out of her life, Jack."

"I'll get her back, Sarah," Posey said. "I promise."

"Don't promise," Sarah said. "Promises can be broken. Swear."

Posey nodded. "I swear."

Sarah sighed and stood up. "I'm going to visit Dale," she said. "I won't be long."

CHAPTER THIRTY

Sarah concluded her hour-long service by saying, "As most of you know, my daughter has been kidnapped by the outlaws Tom Spooner and Pepper Broussard. As they did so, my husband, Dale, was severely wounded. Dale's brother, Deputy Marshal Jack Posey, and his associate, an army scout, will leave this afternoon to pursue the outlaws and bring them to justice and return my daughter home. I would like everybody to bow their heads and say a silent prayer for their success."

The standing-room-only crowd bowed their heads for a moment of silence.

Sarah looked at Posey, and he nodded to her.

After loading their horses onto the boxcar of the three-car train, Posey and Scout walked along the platform to where Sarah, John, and Evan waited.

"John, you look after your mother until we get back," Posey said. "And Evan, you look after John."

Sarah stared at Posey. She reached into her handbag and removed a small doll with golden hair. "This is Erin's favorite doll," she said and gave it to Posey.

Posey nodded, took the doll, and then boarded the train.

"We'll be back," Scout said and followed Posey.

As the only two passengers on the special train, tickets weren't required, but the conductor was on board, as he was in charge of the train.

"We'll be leaving any minute," he said. "It will take us about fourteen hours to reach Cheyenne, so I made sure we have plenty of hot coffee and sandwiches."

"Obliged to you and the railroad," Posey said.

"No thanks necessary, Marshal," the conductor said. "That son of a bitch robbed us three times in two years."

The train slowly moved forward. Posey looked out the window at Sarah, John, and Evan. He made brief eye contact with Sarah, and she nodded at him.

Posey opened his eyes when the door of the

car slammed shut. Outside his window it was dark. In the seat opposite him, Scout yawned.

The conductor rolled a cart to their seats.

"Hot coffee and sandwiches," the conductor said. "Two for each."

Posey dug out his pocket watch and checked the time. It was a few minutes past midnight. "How long to Cheyenne?" he asked.

"I figure we'll arrive around four in the morning," the conductor said. "I'll be back later for the cart," he said and left the car.

Posey took a sandwich and cup of coffee, as did Scout. Thick slices of roast beef between hunks of crusty bread, warm to the touch.

"The railroad people know how to live," Scout said.

"How long do you figure it will take us to reach Buffalo from Cheyenne?" Posey asked.

"Two days and a bit, from the look of the maps," Scout said.

"We'll need to pick up supplies for a week in Cheyenne," Posey said.

"And then some," Scout said.

Posey ate some of his sandwich and washed it down with coffee.

"How do you figure Spooner knew where

to go grab the little girl?" Scout asked.

"We go back to the war, the three of us," Posey said. "I rode with Spooner afterwards for a spell until we parted ways. He must have figured it was me down in Mexico and that I would spare the boy. He must have figured the boy would tell me about the Bighorns. He took the girl to make sure I'd show up, and we'd put an end to it instead of dragging it out."

"Would he really kill that girl if he saw you wasn't alone?"

"Him and Broussard, and not think twice."

"Then he best not see me," Scout said.

The train arrived in Cheyenne a few minutes past four in the morning. A major hub for the railroad expansion west, the city's four thousand residents were mostly asleep. Those who were awake worked for the railroad.

Chief of Railroad Police Jess Stockton and four of his men greeted Posey and Scout on the station platform.

"Marshal Posey, I'm Jess Stockton, Chief of Railroad Police. These are my deputies," Stockton said. "I got a warm office with beds in the back where you can wait for sunrise. My men will tend to your horses."

"It's a mite chilly here this morning," Scout said.

"This is Wyoming," Stockton said. "Every morning here is a mite chilly."

Posey and Scout slept for several hours and awoke around seven in the morning. Stockton had a pot of coffee waiting for them on the Franklin stove in the office.

Posey filled two cups, gave one to Scout, and took a chair behind one of four vacant desks.

"We'll pick up supplies as soon as the general store opens," Posey said. "Let's have another look at the map."

Scout went to his saddlebags in the corner of the office, brought the map to the desk, and spread it out in front of Posey.

"Do you think we need a compass?" Posey asked.

"No," Scout said. "What we need is a plan."

"How are you at night tracking?" Posey asked.

"Don't matter to me," Scout said.

The office door opened and Stockton walked in. "Can I interest you gentlemen in some breakfast?" he asked.

At the restaurant in the lobby of the Hotel

Cheyenne, Posey, Scout, and Stockton had breakfast.

"I'm offering the services of the railroad police," Stockton said. "As Spooner is wanted for train robbery, it makes it my jurisdiction."

"Spooner has kidnapped a young girl. My brother's daughter," Posey said. "If he sees anybody but me, he'll kill her for sure. I don't even know how I am going to hide Scout here, much less a bunch of railroad police."

"I see," Stockton said.

"I been thinking about those cattle they stole that time the boy told us about," Scout said. "He said they rustled them cattle in Casper. That means there has to be a back-door pass in the mountains to his hideout south of Buffalo."

"I go in the front door while you take the back?" Posey said. "It would take some planning."

"It would," Scout admitted.

"If me and some of my men took the back door with your man here, they'd never see us coming," Stockton said.

"It could work," Scout said. "With some planning."

"Got any detailed maps of the Bighorns?" Posey asked Stockton.

Scout traced a path with his finger on a detailed map on Stockton's desk. "From Casper to Buffalo looks about two days' ride and a bit," he said. "The boy put the entrance to Spooner's hideout about here." Scout moved his finger along the map. "Halfway along the red cliffs to a V-notch box canyon."

Stockton examined the map closely. "It's not on the map, this canyon."

"No, it wouldn't be," Scout said. "They probably found it by accident, or maybe the Cheyenne or Crow know about it and showed them the way for a price."

Posey rolled a cigarette, lit it with a wood match, and studied the map.

"I think I can find the box canyon by myself," Posey said. "Scout, if you take Stockton and his men and can find the back door near Casper and give me three days to find the front door, you can come up behind their hideout and wait for me."

"Leave you out there alone?" Scout said. "Spooner could have more than just Broussard with him."

"Not guarding the back door," Posey said. "Spooner probably will have men keeping watch close to the hideout to warn Spooner and not to take me out. He wants that pleasure for himself. I have to go in alone, or Spooner and Broussard will kill the girl for sure. I can't allow that."

"If you don't make it?" Stockton asked.

"Do what you can to save the girl, but don't risk her life," Posey said.

"Say we find the back door of the hideout, how long do we wait for you, and how will we know if you made it?" Stockton asked.

"Find a good place to watch the rear of the cabin from a safe distance and watch for Spooner's men riding in from the north to warn him," Posey said.

Stockton looked at Posey.

"What did you do in the war, Marshal?" Stockton asked.

"Advance scout for Sherman, mostly on his march to the sea," Posey said.

Scout and Stockton stared at Posey.

"And so was Tom Spooner," Posey said. "Why do you think no one has caught him?"

CHAPTER THIRTY-ONE

After a hard day's ride north to Casper, they made camp close to sundown and built a fire to cook hot food.

Posey, Scout, Stockton, and four of his men sat around the campfire and drank coffee while they waited for the food to cook.

"We should reach Casper by early evening tomorrow," Scout said. "I should be able to find that back door by the time you reach Buffalo."

"I'll need two days to find the hideout once I reach Buffalo," Posey said. "When you see Spooner's lookouts come running, you'll know I arrived."

"What makes a man like Tom Spooner do the things he does?" Stockton asked. "You rode with him, Marshal, why?"

Posey sipped some coffee. "When we returned home to our farms in Missouri after the war, we found Rebel sympathizers had murdered our families and burned our homes. We fought a war to save the country and came home to nothing but misery. It turns a man bitter."

Scout and Stockton looked at Posey.

"We set out together to get revenge on those that done it," Posey said. "We took our revenge upon the south, robbing and burning whatever and wherever we could, but after a time I realized there was nobody to take our revenge on, so I went my separate way from Spooner. But old Tom, he just kept at it, and I believe it's because he developed a taste for the bloodshed. I believe he thinks the more blood he sheds, the more he gets even for what was done to him. He doesn't, of course. He is not of right mind. I never met Broussard, but I'd guess he has the same taste for blood as Spooner. I can't guess as to his reasons. Maybe he was just born bad."

"I hear of a boy named Jim Miller who shot and killed both his grandparents when he was just eight years old in Evant, Texas, for no reason," Scout said. "A boy that could do that is like you said, just born bad."

"Wasn't John Wesley Hardin charged with his first murder at the age of sixteen?" Stockton asked.

"Believe he was," Scout said.

"I guess it doesn't really matter how

young they start, sooner or later they all wind up like Wild Bill Hickok," Stockton said.

Hearing the name Hickok brought to Posey's mind Calamity Jane and the sadness she carried in her heart. Wasted life will do that to a person.

"Food's ready, gentlemen, let's eat," Stockton said.

Posey kept his mind blank as he followed Scout's lead. To his right was Stockton and behind them Stockton's men. Conversation wasn't necessary and barely a word was spoken all day.

As they rode, it became clear to Posey that Scout was an incredible tracker. He had an uncanny sense of direction and didn't need to check the sun to keep on path. He could tell the time just by looking at shadows made by the horses or a tree.

Late in the afternoon, Scout pulled up.

"We made good time," Scout said. "Casper is less than an hour to the east. We can resupply and split up in the morning."

"I'll take one of my men into town for supplies," Stockton said. "Marshal, do you want anything particular?"

"Cornbread, if they have it, and tobacco and paper. I'm running low," Posey said.

■ ■ ■ ■

Around a campfire, Stockton opened the bottle of bourbon whiskey he picked up in Casper and added an ounce to each coffee cup.

"The shopkeeper said this whiskey came all the way from Kentucky," Stockton said. "When men ride together on a mission like we are now, they deserve a decent drink to end the night with."

Posey sipped his bourbon-laced coffee.

"Have you men ever heard of tequila?" he asked.

After breakfast, they broke camp and shook hands.

"Give me four days, and keep watch on the back door," Posey said.

"You'll have it," Scout said.

Posey pulled the Sharps rifle from his saddle and tossed it to Scout. "Are you any good with this?" he asked.

"Not so good as you, but I can hold my own," Scout said.

"You'll need this then," Posey said and tossed Scout the box of Sharps ammunition.

Scout nodded. "Good luck, Marshal."

"You too," Posey said and mounted his horse.

CHAPTER THIRTY-TWO

Posey kept his mind free of outside thoughts as he rode north toward Buffalo. There wasn't room for thoughts of Pilar, or anything else for that matter, except for Tom Spooner and Pepper Broussard.

Posey knew he would be riding into a trap. He knew Spooner and how the man acted and thought. He relied upon his army training to plan his jobs and escapes. He was a lot like Jesse and Frank James in that regard. Guerrilla warfare with a planned route of escape.

It was the advantage of surprise Spooner relied upon. His last job in Texas, robbing the railroad payroll, probably took a month or more of planning the attack and the escape to Nuevo.

Once Posey fouled his escape route, Spooner realized that to successfully pull off the payroll robbery, he needed to sacrifice his own men. And he did so willingly.

Word must have reached him somehow that Posey was paroled and working for his brother and that it was Posey in Nuevo, so in order to set a trap for him, Spooner needed an edge.

Always have an edge against your opponent. In terrain, the high ground, superior numbers, and the element of a surprise attack at dawn; battles are won and lost on an edge.

That's how Jesse James was defeated in Minnesota. He lost his edge when the entire town turned out to be armed and ready to fight. Lose your edge and lose the fight.

Spooner's edge was Erin.

He knew Posey would never do anything to endanger the life of Erin.

The sun was hot on his back, and he paused briefly to rest the horse and eat a cold lunch of cornbread, jerky, and water.

After eating, he rolled a cigarette from the fresh tobacco pouch and smoked in the shade of a tall tree.

Finished with the cigarette, he went to the horse and gently rubbed his powerful neck for a few moments.

"It occurs to me that after all the riding we've done together, I failed to give you a proper name," Posey said. "Well, you got the heart of a lion and the tenacity of a bear.

I'll call you Bear, how's that?"

Responding to Posey's voice and touch, the newly named Bear turned his neck and looked at him.

"Bear it is," Posey said and mounted the saddle.

Late in the afternoon, Posey, riding in a northwest direction, noticed a group of Indians in the high ground to his left. They followed him but kept their distance. They were too far away for him to identify what tribe they belonged to, but if they meant him harm, they would have done so already.

Near dusk, Posey decided to make camp for the night. He built a large fire and put on coffee, bacon, and beans. While the food cooked, he hobbled Bear and gave him a good brushing.

Then he sat with a cup of coffee and a cigarette and waited.

The Indians arrived and stopped fifty feet in front of the fire. One dismounted and approached Posey.

Posey stood.

As the Indian came into the light of the fire, Posey saw he was a handsome man and wearing the shirt of an army sergeant.

"I am White Buffalo of the North Cheyenne and scout for the soldiers at Miles

City," White Buffalo said. "We set out a month ago on patrol."

"You're a long way from home," Posey said.

"I am," White Buffalo said.

"I am called Jack Posey," Posey said.

"You wear the star of the lawman," White Buffalo said.

"I do," Posey said. "Federal marshal. Will you sit and share a meal with me? I have fresh cornbread."

White Buffalo sat before the fire, and Posey filled two plates with beans, bacon, and cornbread and gave one plate to White Buffalo.

"Do you drink coffee?" Posey asked.

"Do you have sugar?"

"I do."

"Then I drink coffee," White Buffalo said.

Posey filled a spare cup with coffee, added some sugar, and gave the cup to White Buffalo.

"I have seen strange things today," White Buffalo said.

"What have you seen?" Posey asked.

"Men riding west into the mountains led by a man who wears the shirt of an army scout," White Buffalo said. "And I have seen you riding alone."

"Those men are my friends," Posey said.

330

"They are also lawmen. We are tracking some very bad men into the mountains."

"What have these men done?"

"Have you heard of the outlaw Tom Spooner?"

"I have heard of this man."

"He has killed many innocent men, women, and children and robbed many banks and trains," Posey said. "Now he has kidnapped a young girl, and I am trying to save her. Do you know this word, kidnapped?"

White Buffalo shook his head.

"It means stolen," Posey said.

"To what end?" White Buffalo asked.

"He's running from the law, and he knows we won't do anything to risk the young girl's life," Posey said. "We call a person taken like that a hostage."

"That's why you left the others and ride alone?"

"Yes. If Spooner sees more than one rider, he has said he will kill the girl."

"Will he?"

"Oh, yeah."

"Where is he hiding?"

"Supposedly some secret pass no one knows about," Posey said. "I have reason to believe I can find it."

"I have heard of this pass, but have never

seen it," White Buffalo said. "The Crow or Sioux may know where it is."

"I haven't got time to find some Crow or Sioux and ask them," Posey said.

"Men can sometimes be wretched things," White Buffalo said.

"I won't argue that point," Posey said.

"Have you tobacco, Jack Posey?"

"I have, but no pipe," Posey said.

White Buffalo removed a pipe from his shirt pocket and Posey passed him the tobacco pouch. After stuffing the pipe, White Buffalo returned the pouch to Posey, who rolled a cigarette.

"I will see you again, Jack Posey," White Buffalo said.

He stood, as did Posey, and they shook hands.

The following day, Posey rode a hard thirty miles and reached west of Buffalo just before sunset.

He made camp about a mile west of town and could see dots of lights on the horizon. After building a fire and putting on some food, he gave Bear a good brushing and fed him some grain.

Posey ate and turned in early and as he watched the stars come out and the moon rise, he thought of White Buffalo's words.

"Men can sometimes be wretched things."

"I'm counting on it," Posey said aloud and closed his eyes.

Chapter Thirty-Three

"I know I shouldn't, but you'll need the extra strength for today's haul," Posey told Bear as he fed him grain.

While Bear ate the grain, Posey had breakfast and waited for the sun to fully rise.

When day broke, he packed up, saddled Bear, and rode west into the foothills of the Bighorn Mountains.

The hills between the mountains were lush and rolling as Posey rode west toward higher ground. He rode until noon and rested Bear while he ate a cold lunch of cornbread, jerky, and water.

The afternoon was spent traveling hills closer to the mountains until, close to dusk, he found the red cliffs Evan had described.

Mountains as high as thirteen thousand feet loomed over Posey and Bear as Posey stopped to make evening camp.

Supper was beans, bacon, and cornbread with a few sticks of jerky and coffee.

After eating, when the moon was up, Posey brushed Bear while he grazed on tall sweet grass.

Bear turned his neck to nuzzle Posey.

"Yeah, I'm growing right fond of you, too," Posey said.

Once Bear was hobbled for the night, Posey rolled a cigarette and used his saddle to lean against as he watched the stars and moon.

"All those wasted years," he said aloud, and was surprised to hear his own voice.

At daybreak, Posey rode southwest along the red cliffs, searching for the V-notch described by Evan.

Around noon, off in the distance, he spotted a V-notch canyon in the mountains.

He rested Bear for an hour and let him graze as much as he wanted. Posey ate some cornbread with water in the shade of a tree.

He studied the mountains and shapes of the cliffs, the peaks and valleys in the distance. He calculated he would reach the V-notch by sundown.

Back in the saddle, Posey recalled many of the raids he and Spooner rode on during the war and after.

During the war, Posey and Spooner followed orders. They believed in the cause of preserving the Union and ending slavery. So when they were called upon to kill in the line of duty, Posey knew there was a greater good behind his actions.

After the war, when revenge became the motive for their actions, Posey knew what he was doing was the wrong course of action, but he was filled with hate and bitterness toward the country he fought to preserve, the country that allowed his parents and sister to be butchered and murdered.

When he and Spooner split ways, it was because Posey had enough of bloodshed in his still young life and realized that blood for blood would never return his parents and sister to life.

Seeking revenge had the opposite effect on Spooner. Rather than ease the pain, it only made it worse.

Posey had twenty-two thousand dollars in gold coins when he and Spooner went their separate ways. He managed to make it to the farm and bury the money in the field. There was nothing left of the house and barn, and the fields were untouched and overgrown with weeds.

He left with the feeling of wasted life in his gut, and that feeling had stayed with him ever since, much the way it did with Jane.

He worked as a cowboy, working ranches

and cattle drives for twenty-five dollars a month as a way to lose himself. Spooner must have spent some time and money locating him and arranging for the false betrayal that had landed Posey in Yuma. He must have felt threatened that one day Posey would turn himself in and point a finger at Spooner.

He wasn't entirely wrong in that notion. Posey was ready to turn himself in when the law caught up with him, but he would never have betrayed Spooner.

And while he rotted in Yuma, Posey feared in his gut that his wasted life would always be there, like a sickness there was no cure for. When Dale showed up and offered the pardon in exchange for his help capturing Spooner, Posey took the deal, but not because he wanted to help his brother. Rather, as he did after the war, he wanted revenge, and his heart went pitch-black.

Until he met Pilar.

And she gave him hope.

Close to sundown, Posey made camp about a mile from the V-notch canyon.

The thing to do, he told himself as he built a fire and put on some food to cook, was not to think about Pilar.

The way to survive a war was to not think about what you left behind. To not miss home and loved ones. To put it behind you and focus only on what you needed to do to stay alive.

Because if you didn't stay alive, what was the point?

Posey ate while watching the V-notch slowly fade to darkness with the setting sun.

CHAPTER THIRTY-FOUR

The entrance to the canyon was several hundred yards across with mountains on each side that cast the canyon floor in shadow.

By noon, the canyon had started to narrow, as Evan said it would. Posey paused for an hour to rest Bear and eat a cold lunch.

As he sat with his back against the saddle, he studied the cliffs and peaks on both sides of the valley.

Some of the peaks rose to three thousand feet or more in height.

From the top looking down, a lookout would not be able to see a rider. The angle was too steep.

For Spooner's lookouts to be effective, they would have to be on a shorter peak, be able to have a view of the floor below, and be within a few minutes' ride of Spooner in order to warn him.

A mile, two at most to reach Spooner.

The ideal spot for a lookout was deeper into the canyon.

Posey rode until sunset and the next day until early afternoon, when the canyon began to funnel as the boy described.

Posey dismounted and studied the cliffs and peaks on both sides of him.

Elevation of two thousand or more feet high with a narrow view of the canyon floor. Up ahead, the peaks were shorter, gentler, and a lookout would be able to see a rider coming.

"We're close," Posey told Bear as he rubbed his neck. "We'll get a bit closer and go in come morning."

After Posey had ridden several hours, the canyon narrowed to just a few hundred feet across. The cliff and peaks were a thousand feet high or less. Sunlight reached the sides of the canyon wall on Posey's right.

He dismounted and walked Bear for a mile or more and then stopped.

The canyon floor was less than a hundred feet across. The right wall was bathed in sun, the left in shadow. Directly ahead, the canyon curved to the left and the path wasn't visible.

He walked Bear to some tall grass, dug

out the leather strips from a saddlebag, and hobbled him.

"I won't be long," Posey told Bear. "Eat some grass and grab a nap while I'm gone."

Posey removed the Winchester from the saddle sleeve and walked to the shadowy cliff on his left. The climb wasn't sheer, but was at least a thousand feet. The lookouts would be on the cliff where the sun was at their back so they could see the canyon floor without glare in their faces.

The climb was slow and somewhat cumbersome. After five hundred feet or so, Posey took a five-minute break. He checked his pocket watch. It was just short of eleven-thirty in the morning.

The next five hundred feet to the top took a bit longer, as it was sheerer with softer dirt, and he backslid a few times.

Finally, Posey reached the flat plateau and rolled onto his back to catch his breath.

He finally sat up close to the edge, looked down, and then stood up. He could see Bear eating some grass.

Posey turned away from the edge, walked about a hundred feet, and turned to his right. He went about a mile before he spotted a man standing close to the edge of the cliff. Two horses were hobbled about fifty feet to the man's left.

He walked to within a hundred feet of the man. Behind a tree, Posey removed his boots and crept up on the man from behind.

The man was talking to another man who was prone on the ground on a blanket.

With the sun at his back, Posey stealthily moved to within six feet of the man standing near the edge.

"When we done with this lookout foolishness, we'll ride over to Buffalo and get us a room, a bottle, and a couple of five-dollar whores and not come up for air for at least a week," the man said.

"What about your ranch?" the man on the ground said.

"Cows is cows. They can wait," the man said. "If a man got the need to wiggle his bean, the cows can wait."

Posey cocked the lever of the Winchester and said, "If you ever want to wiggle your bean again, you'll remove that Schofield from your holster nice and slow and toss it to the ground."

The man froze in place.

The man in the blanket sat up.

"You in the bedroll, nobody said you could move. Don't even twitch or you'll get it first," Posey said.

"I ain't armed," the man in the blanket said. "My holster is over by my saddle."

With his back still to Posey, the other man said, "What's this about, mister? We done no wrong. Me and my friend here are just —"

"I know what you're doing," Posey said. "I'm the one you're keeping watch for. Now be smart and drop the Schofield."

The man brought his right hand to the butt of his Schofield pistol.

"Now ease it out and toss it to the ground," Posey said.

"You got us all wrong, mister," the man said. "We're cowpunchers."

"Camping out on the edge of a cliff in the middle of nowhere?" Posey said. "Lose the Schofield, and I won't tell you again."

Posey watched the man's right hand. It twitched slightly. The man's right shoulder dipped and tightened slightly.

Posey held the Winchester high so that the stock faced the man. When the man reached for the Schofield and spun around, Posey smashed him in the face with the butt of the Winchester.

The man stumbled backward, tripped over the legs of the man in the blanket, and went over the cliff backwards. He screamed on the way down, and after a few seconds went silent.

Posey sighed.

"Well, that didn't go as planned," he said.

"Don't kill me, mister," the man in the blanket said.

"Oh, shut up," Posey said.

"Can I put my boots on and stand up?"

"Go ahead," Posey said.

The man grabbed his boots, put them on, and stood up.

"Gosh, mister, you killed my friend."

"I didn't plan on him being so stupid, and he tripped over your legs anyway," Posey said. He looked at the man closer and realized he was a boy, not much older than Evan.

"How old are you?" Posey asked.

"Sixteen."

"Sixteen. What's your name, son?"

"Parker. Robert Parker."

"Got any grub, Robert Parker?"

"Some."

"Make a fire and cook some of it," Posey said.

Parker went to the ashes of a previous fire and tossed in some sticks from a stacked bundle.

"Got coffee?"

"Yes, sir," Parker said and noticed Posey's badge. "I mean. Marshal."

"What was his name, your misguided friend?"

"Mike Cassidy. What's misguided mean?"

"Another way of saying foolish. I'll note his name when I bury him later," Posey said. "Go on and make a fire while I get my boots."

Parker proved handy around a campfire and served up scrambled eggs with bacon and beans with coffee.

"Where'd you get the fresh eggs?" Posey asked.

"Chickens." Parker grinned. He was a handsome kid with dark hair and eyes and a stout build.

"And the chickens?"

"There's a mess of them at the cabin," Parker said. "A rooster, too."

"So what are you doing hooked up with the likes of Spooner and Broussard?" Posey asked. "You're just a kid, for God's sake."

"Back home in Utah, my folks is Mormons and real poor," Parker said. "They sent me to work on ranches in the area, and I went to work for Mister Cassidy. Course, he spent most of his time stealing other ranchers' cattle than raise his own. We was in Miles City a while back and met Mister Spooner, and he asked us to watch his cattle at this cabin he had in the mountains. He was gone almost a month."

"And he came back and asked you to stand watch for me?"

"He didn't say the law," Parker said. "He said someone he used to ride with had a grudge against him and we was to warn him right away when we saw you coming. He paid me fifty dollars in gold."

"And when the shooting starts?" Posey asked. "What good is your fifty dollars in gold to you?"

"I got nothing to do with no shooting," Parker said. "My gun is an old Navy Colt. Belongs to my father. It's cap and ball, and half the time the powder's wet."

Posey nodded toward the hobbled horses. "They stolen?"

"Mine ain't. Can't speak for Mike's."

"Now listen to me carefully," Posey said. "Do you want to go to jail?"

"No sir, Marshal."

"Pack up your gear, get on your horse and find the trail out of here that leads to Casper, and then keep going," Posey said. "You seem like a smart kid, and crime is no way to spend your life."

"What about Mike's horse?"

"I'll cut him loose," Posey said. "It's probably stolen anyway. Take what gear of his you need and leave the rest."

Parker nodded. "Are you going after Mr.

Spooner and the other fellow?"

"I am. How far to the cabin?"

"There's no way to get your horse up here except at the end of the canyon trail," Parker said. "That's about two miles from here. Then you turn to the left and ride about another mile or so. You'll see it plain as day."

"Okay, Robert Parker, pack up your gear and get moving," Posey said.

Parker gathered his gear and saddled his horse. He wore a sheepish grin as he stood before Posey.

"Sorry for any trouble I caused, Marshal," he said. "It weren't my intent."

Despite the fact that Parker was to warn Spooner of his coming, Posey liked the boy.

"Your friends call you Bob?" Posey asked.

"Naw. They call me Butch, on account I once worked in a butcher shop in Utah."

"Okay, Butch, get going," Posey said.

Posey waited until Parker was well out of view, then went to Cassidy's horse, removed the bit, and cut him loose.

"Go on now, get going," Posey said, and smacked him on the rump.

As the horse ran away, Posey picked up Cassidy's saddle and gear, carried it to the cliff, and tossed it over.

"Might as well bury it with the rest of you," he said.

■ ■ ■ ■

Bear was asleep when Posey returned and unhobbled him.

"Come on," Posey said and led Bear by the reins. "We have a body to bury."

It was well after dark by the time Posey tossed the last shovelful of dirt on Cassidy's gravesite. He had paused to build a fire and put on some food before finishing digging the grave, and when he sat against his saddle to eat, he felt exhaustion wash over him.

Before he turned in, Posey fed Bear grain and brushed his coat.

"I don't know what will happen tomorrow, but whatever happens, I'll be sure to keep you out of the line of fire," Posey said.

Bear turned and looked at Posey.

"You're welcome," Posey said.

CHAPTER THIRTY-FIVE

After a hot breakfast of bacon, beans, and the last bit of cornbread, Posey saddled Bear and rode cautiously along the canyon floor as directed by Parker. The morning sun wasn't high enough yet, and he rode in shadows.

Last night had been a restless night full of bad dreams and memories.

And lies.

He lied to Dale about his reasons for accepting the pardon and badge.

He lied to Jane to use her to find Spooner.

He lied to Belle Starr for the same reason.

He even lied to that old buzzard, Judge Bean.

And he lied to Pilar, although when he did tell her the truth, it seemed to make no difference to her.

Or to Dale, for that matter.

Maybe that was how love was supposed to be. A person can see the bad in another person and still love him for what good there was.

Except that Posey didn't know what good Pilar or Dale saw in him.

When he did sleep, he dreamt about the farm and the war. How he carried the guilt around for not being there when his parents and sister were murdered even though the truth was that, had he been there, he would have been murdered right alongside them.

The guilt, he realized, was not born of the idea that they were murdered senselessly, but that he lived while they died.

Since the war, he carried that guilt around on his back like it was a sack of adobe bricks.

Pilar took that sack and set it to the ground.

And during his restless night, he awoke and realized that he didn't want to die without seeing her one last time.

Bear held up as if he sensed something ahead he didn't want to encounter.

Posey snapped out of his daydream and realized they had come to the end of the narrow pass in the canyon.

"Right," Posey said and dismounted. He took the reins and walked Bear up a softly rolling hill and onto a lush valley.

"So far that kid's telling the truth," Posey

said as he mounted the saddle. "Let's find out."

After about a half mile, Posey spotted a cabin in the distance.

He dismounted and dug the binoculars out of the saddlebags. Using the saddle to rest the binoculars on, Posey scanned the cabin. It was large with a deep front porch. The porch had no railing. A large window flanked each side of the door. Smoke rose up from the chimney.

To the left of the cabin and directly behind it was a small corral with two horses in it.

"Let's get a bit closer," Posey told Bear as he mounted the saddle.

About three hundred feet to the left of the cabin, Posey dismounted and used the binoculars for a closer look through the windows.

The man who had to be Pepper Broussard was seated at a table in the left side of the cabin. He wore his long underwear and appeared to be drinking coffee. There was no sign of Spooner or Erin in either window.

Sunlight reflected off the open window on the right side.

"Glass," Posey said softly. "The cabin has glass windows."

He put the binoculars away and walked Bear to within two hundred feet of the cabin. He could see Broussard still drinking. Some chickens pecked at the ground beside the cabin.

Posey rubbed Bear's neck. "You wait for me here," he whispered.

Leaving Bear, Posey walked directly in front of the window to the right of the door from a distance of about two hundred feet. From that angle, Broussard was no longer visible.

Posey stood perfectly still and closed his eyes for a brief moment. He heard Belle Starr's voice in his head.

"You'd be better off waltzing with the devil."

Posey opened his eyes. "I prefer a two-step," he said.

He took a deep breath and exhaled slowly, and then broke into a hard run directly toward the cabin. At the porch, he leapt onto it, covered his face with his arms, and crashed through the right-side window.

As he landed on the other side, he grabbed his Colt, rolled, and quickly stood up just as Spooner ran out the back door.

Pepper Broussard sat calmly sipping his coffee at a table. He looked at Posey. The long scar on his cheek moved as he spoke.

"You'd be Jack Posey," Broussard said.

"And you're Pepper Broussard," Posey said.

"I am," Broussard said. He sipped some coffee and grinned at Posey. His teeth were yellow and foul-looking.

"I see Spooner didn't stick around," Posey said.

"Old Tom," Broussard said. "I expected no less from him. Now what?"

Posey looked at the holster hanging from a hook on the wall beside the table.

"Stand up and put your gun belt on," Posey said.

"Tom said you had no stomach for killing in cold blood," Broussard said. "Guess he was right."

"Do it," Posey said.

"You sure?" Broussard grinned.

"Do it," Posey said again.

Broussard slid his chair back and slowly stood up. He smirked as he reached for his holster. "Tom said they used to call you Lightning Jack in the old days," he said.

"I never liked that name," Posey said.

Slowly, carefully, Broussard strapped on his holster.

"I see you carry the likeness of Doc Holliday's nickel-plated Colt," Posey said.

"You'll see it soon enough," Broussard said.

Posey holstered his Colt. "Show it to me," he said.

Broussard grinned his yellow, rotten grin.

A moment of calm stillness passed. Neither man moved a muscle. With the table between them, they were separated by about twelve feet, a distance impossible to miss from.

Posey saw Broussard's shoulder twitch and both men reached for their guns. Two shots fired simultaneously sounded as one.

Broussard's shot entered Posey's lower, left abdomen and made a clean exit wound. He turned on impact and immediately righted himself.

Posey's shot struck Broussard a few inches to the left of his heart. He fell backwards to the floor.

Posey walked forward and looked behind the table. Broussard was on his back still holding onto his nickel-plated Colt. He looked at Posey and grunted loudly as he rolled onto his side.

"You son of a bitch," Broussard said and cocked his Colt. "You go to hell."

Posey shot Broussard a second time in the chest, and Broussard dropped his gun and hit the floor.

"You first," Posey said.

Broussard died looking at the ceiling.

Posey opened the loading gate, replaced

the two spent rounds, then went to the back door.

In the distance, Spooner was on his horse and at least a thousand yards away. Erin was in the saddle with him.

Bleeding heavily from his wound, Posey went outside to the porch. He whistled to Bear, and the horse trotted over to him.

"We got some riding to do," Posey said and grunted in pain as he mounted the saddle.

With a hard yank on the reins, Bear took off running. Behind the house, Spooner was still in sight and riding hard.

Posey tugged the reins, and Bear opened his stride up full. He ran for a full five minutes without breaking stride, and Posey saw they had gained on Spooner.

Spooner always like to ride a light horse built for short bursts of speed, but what a light horse had in speed, it lacked in endurance.

Bear started to sweat and his nostrils flared, but he kept his stride and gave Posey his all.

The gap closed.

Spooner's horse tired badly.

"You got him, Bear," Posey said. "Don't let him get away."

Bear kept his pace, and Posey ignored the

hot pain in his side. Soon the gap closed to just several hundred feet.

Then Spooner did the unexpected. He pulled his horse to a complete stop, turned him around, and faced Posey.

Posey tugged his reins and slowed Bear until fifty feet separated them.

Erin was in front of Spooner on the saddle. He dismounted, yanked her down, drew his gun, and stuck it against her head.

Erin was frightened into shock and stood motionless.

"I will splatter this girl's brains to the winds, Jack," Spooner said. "And you know I'll do what I say."

"Let the girl go, Tom. She's done you no harm," Posey said.

"The hell you say," Spooner said. "Climb down off that horse and toss the Colt."

Posey dismounted and moved away from Bear.

"The Colt," Spooner said.

Posey opened his gun belt and dropped it to the ground.

"Now let her go, Tom," Posey said.

"In time," Spooner said.

"She's just a child, Tom."

"I know that, but I will do what I have to do," Spooner said. "I see you took Pepper. I told him you could, but he wouldn't listen."

"He was fast, Tom. Very fast."

"Not fast enough," Spooner said. "Although I see he got one in before he died. What about my lookouts?"

"Killed one. The other was just a boy. I let him go."

"I didn't figure on you taking my lookouts, but you always was smart, weren't you, Jack."

"Why don't you be smart, Tom, and let the girl go," Posey said.

"When she's of no more use," Spooner said.

"Let her go, and I won't come after you," Posey said. "All I want is the girl."

"That's too thin a promise, Jack," Spooner said. "I think I'll just hold on to her for a while longer."

"Why did you set me up, Tom? I would not have told the law about you."

"I couldn't trust you wouldn't turn on me if the law caught up with you," Spooner said. "Make yourself a deal at my expense. And I see by that badge you did just that."

"I sat in Yuma two years and never said a word," Posey said. "My brother got me out on a pardon."

"I heard that and knew right away you'd come looking for me," Spooner said. "I was near Tucson when they let you out. I planned that payroll job in Texas and figured to spend six months in Mexico. That was you killed my men, wasn't it Jack?"

Posey nodded.

"Revenge on old Tom, is it? But old Tom has the upper hand now, don't he?" Spooner said and cocked his gun.

"Tom, don't," Posey said. "Shoot me if you have to, but not the girl."

"Now that's an idea," Spooner said.

He aimed his gun at Posey. Erin came to life and kicked him in the leg.

"Damn child," Spooner said and flung Erin to the ground.

Posey stared at Spooner and looked into his eyes. The man was insane with his hatred and bloodlust.

"I will kill you, Jack, and then for the fun of it I will kill this child," Spooner said.

He pulled the trigger and the bullet tore a hole in Posey's left shoulder. Posey fell to one knee, looked at Spooner, and then stood up.

"I forgot how strong you are, Jack," Spooner said. "Two holes in you and still on your feet."

"Erin, run," Posey shouted.

Erin stared at Posey.

Spooner cocked his gun, aimed, and fired. The bullet struck Posey in the left rib cage and he fell to the ground.

Spooner chuckled as he walked toward Posey.

"We had us a time once, Jack," he said.

Spooner cocked his gun and aimed it at Posey.

"But that party is over," he said.

Posey looked up at Spooner.

"Bye, Jack," Spooner said.

Posey heard a whizzing sound and a large hole appeared in Spooner's chest. Two seconds later, the crack of the Sharps rifle echoed loudly as Spooner fell to his knees.

"Jesus," Spooner said.

Posey reached for his holster and grabbed his Colt. He cocked the hammer, aimed it at Spooner, and shot him in the chest. As Spooner fell dead to the ground, Posey said, "Don't count on meeting him any time soon."

Then, light-headed and weak, Posey dropped the Colt, rolled onto his back, and heard Erin run to him.

"Uncle Jack," she cried.

"Are you hurt?" Posey asked.

"No."

"Good."

"Uncle Jack, men are coming."

"That would be Scout," Posey said. "He's a good man. You listen to him."

Posey closed his eyes and Erin screamed, "Uncle Jack."

Erin knelt beside Posey as Scout, Stockton, and the others raced to a stop beside Posey. They quickly dismounted and went to his side.

"He's still alive," Scout said. "Rip open his shirt. Quick."

As Stockton ripped open Posey's shirt, Scout went for a bottle of whiskey in his saddlebags. He pulled the cork and poured whiskey onto Posey's wounds. "They got a doctor at Buffalo?" he asked.

"A good one I hear," Stockton said.

"Make some mud, quick," Scout said.

Stockton's men made mud from canteen water and scooped it onto a tin plate from their gear. Scout poured half the bottle of whiskey into the mud, mixed it up, and then stuck the whiskey-laced mud into Posey's wounds.

"Put him on my horse and tie his hands to the saddle horn," Scout said.

As Stockton's men lifted Posey and placed him on Scout's horse, Scout and Stockton went to Erin.

Scout knelt before her.

"I'll get him to Buffalo, to the doctor," Scout said. "You'll follow with Mr. Stockton here and the others."

"My Uncle Jack is very brave," Erin said.

Scout grinned. "He is that," he said.

"Come with me, honey," Stockton said and took Erin's hand.

Scout went to his horse and mounted the saddle behind the unconscious Posey.

"See you in Buffalo," Scout said and yanked hard on the reins.

CHAPTER THIRTY-SIX

Scout ran his horse hard along the canyon floor toward the town of Buffalo. The horse had no quit in him and gave it his all for several hours. But even the best of horses will tire if forced to run long enough. By early afternoon Scout's horse, covered in sweat and steam, began to lose pace.

"We're almost out of the canyon," Scout said to his horse. "Just give me a little more."

The horse responded and gave Scout what little he had left and they cleared the canyon. Soon the Bighorn Mountains were behind them. They raced across the open, flat ground for another mile, but exhausted, the horse began to falter and slow and Scout was forced to stop.

He dismounted and checked his horse. A thick layer of salty sweat covered his chest and legs, and to force him to run any more was to kill him.

Scout checked Posey. Remarkably the man was still alive, though barely. Scout wasn't sure how far it was to Buffalo, but he knew it must be at least another twenty miles. Scout rubbed his horse's neck and brushed away salty foam.

"Won't make another twenty feet," Scout said.

He looked at the band of Cheyenne Indians that appeared on his right. They were led by a Cheyenne wearing the shirt of an army scout.

The group of Cheyenne surrounded Scout, and the one wearing the shirt of an army scout dismounted.

"I am White Buffalo," he said. "That is Marshal Jack Posey?"

"It is."

"Is he alive?"

"For now, but I have to get him to the doctor in Buffalo or he won't be."

White Buffalo looked at Scout's horse. "You won't make it."

"Appears not."

White Buffalo looked at his men and spoke to them in Cheyenne. Several dismounted, went to Scout's horse, untied Posey's hands, and carried him to White Buffalo's horse.

"Did he save the little girl?" White Buffalo asked.

"Yes," Scout said.

"I figured he would," White Buffalo said. "Don't ride that horse again today."

With a yank of the reins, White Buffalo's horse took off running and was quickly followed by his men.

"Damnedest thing I ever saw," Scout said.

Hours later, when Stockton and his men caught up with him, Scout had a campfire going with hot food cooking.

Erin was on Stockton's horse, and he gently lowered her to the ground. Bear was in tow behind Stockton's men.

"Where's the marshal?" Stockton said.

"Damnedest thing I ever saw," Scout said.

CHAPTER THIRTY-SEVEN

When Posey opened his eyes, he was in a bed. Across the dimly lit room, Sarah and Erin were seated in chairs.

Sarah was knitting. Erin was holding the yarn.

"What are you knitting?" Posey asked in a soft, raspy voice.

Sarah and Erin looked at him and burst into tears.

"Well, if knitting upsets you so, I suggest you stop," Posey said, which made them cry even harder.

"Would you females quit your crying and tell me what's going on?" Posey asked.

It took a few moments for Sarah and Erin to compose themselves, but finally they stopped crying and Sarah said, "After you . . ."

"After you killed the outlaw Tom Spooner, Mr. Scout showed up and put you on his horse," Erin said. "He said he'd ride you to

Buffalo, which is where we are right now."

"I see," Posey said.

"Only his horse played out and he didn't make it," Erin said. "You would have died for sure, Uncle Jack, if the Cheyenne Indian scout called White Buffalo didn't come along and take you the rest of the way."

"White Buffalo, huh?" Posey said.

"Yes, sir," Erin said. "He looks real mean, but he ain't."

"He isn't real mean, Erin," Sarah said.

"That's what I said," Erin said.

"No, you said . . . never mind," Sarah said. "Go fetch the doctor and tell him your uncle is awake."

"Be right back, Uncle Jack," Erin said and dashed out of the room.

Posey looked at Sarah. "Dale?"

"At the hospital in Minneapolis," Sarah said. "They saved his leg. He might have a slight limp they said, but he'll be fine in a couple of months."

"Good. God I'm hungry."

"You've been asleep for three days; you ought to be," Sarah said.

"Three days, huh?"

Sarah stood up, walked to the bed, and took Posey's right hand in hers.

"Thank you, Jack," she said softly and started to cry again.

CHAPTER THIRTY-EIGHT

The fall harvest was backbreaking work. Nine or ten hours a day in the sun spent with a scythe in your hands until they were swollen and bleeding.

Jose and Pilar worked the scythe, while Roberto and Carlos gathered the fallen wheat and loaded it into the cart.

They averaged four cartloads a day for the past week.

Pilar wore her man clothes with thick gloves on her hands and worked tirelessly. Her hair was tucked under her Stetson hat to keep the sun off her face. She didn't talk much these days since the marshal left.

She kept busy on the farm, taking the corn and wheat to the mill, and did more work than she had to. Even after dark she kept busy, washing clothes and cleaning.

She rarely smiled much anymore.

Jose set the scythe down, went to the cart, and dipped the ladle into the water bucket.

He took a sip, then removed his hat and poured the rest over his head. He replaced the ladle and noticed something in the distance.

A black dot on the horizon.

His eyesight wasn't as good as it used to be, that was true, but it wasn't so poor either, and he could see just fine at distances. He focused on the dot, and it grew larger.

Then he recognized the dot for what it was.

Jose turned from the cart and looked at Pilar.

"Pilar, take the horse and ride home and change your clothes," Jose said in Spanish. "Go quickly."

Pilar looked at her father. "Why, Papa?" she asked in Spanish.

"Your husband is coming," Jose said.

ABOUT THE AUTHOR

Ethan J. Wolfe is the author of the western novels *The Last Ride, The Regulator, The Range War of '82, Murphy's Law, Silver Moon Rising, All the Queen's Men,* and *One If by Land.*

The employees of Thorndike Press hope you have enjoyed this Large Print book. All our Thorndike, Wheeler, and Kennebec Large Print titles are designed for easy reading, and all our books are made to last. Other Thorndike Press Large Print books are available at your library, through selected bookstores, or directly from us.

For information about titles, please call:
(800) 223-1244

or visit our Web site at:
http://gale.cengage.com/thorndike

To share your comments, please write:
Publisher
Thorndike Press
10 Water St., Suite 310
Waterville, ME 04901